BURIED SECRETS

BURIED SECRETS

A Melissa Mack Adventure
Book Two

J.S. ANDERSEN

Idea Creations Press
www.ideacreationspress.com

 Idea Creations Press
www.ideacreationspress.com

Copyright © J.S. Andersen, 2024.

All rights reserved. No part of this book may be reproduced or transmitted in any form or by any means, electronic or mechanical, including photocopying, recording, or by an information storage and retrieval system, without permission in writing from the author.

This is a work of fiction. Any resemblance of characters to actual persons, living or dead, is purely coincidental.

ISBN: 978-1948804271

I dedicate this book to my mom, who never gave up on me. I know she's smiling down on me from heaven, (January 29, 2022) along with my dad, (March 11, 2008).

A big thanks to the hard-working editors JoEllen Claypool and Kathryn Jones.

And I cannot forget to thank Douglas and Kathryn Jones, at Idea Creations Press, for setting up my book, book cover, and adding the final touches to my story.

Nampa is an actual city in Idaho and the historical information is accurate, including the underground tunnels and the legacy of Bigfoot.

Murphey is also an actual town in Idaho. As stated in the story, the population is small and more like a ghost town. There is no county gymnastics team and BF Café. The Snake River does run by Murphy, but I adjusted its layout to fit the story. Amtrak also does not run by Murphey. I did add lots of trees. In a high desert area, forests aren't common until you reach higher altitude.

Buried Secrets

The Snake River roared against the rugged boulders as its waves crashed with relentless energy. For fifteen-year-old Melissa "Missy" Mack, the scene mirrored her own life—dynamic, unpredictable, and brimming with excitement.

As a sophomore at Nampa High School, Missy's days were a whirlwind of activity. The halls echoed with teenage chatter, lockers slammed in a rhythmic dance, and friendships blossomed like wildflowers in an untamed field. Yet, one aspect of her life felt less exhilarating: her relationship with Brandon Miller, the enigmatic junior with a magnetic smile.

Missy and Brandon dated for a year, but the initial two weeks of school were turbulent. Like a fading star, he drifted away, leaving her to ponder the change. Was it the pressures of high school, or perhaps something deeper—an unspoken rift between them?

Their shared neighborhood should have made their connection stronger. Instead, it only intensified the ache. Despite residing across the neighborhood, she knew Brandon's football practice schedule. With each glimpse from the window facing the road from the back of her house as he drove by in his truck, she wondered why he avoided her. Was it a secret he couldn't share, or had their connection simply unraveled?

"So much for a boyfriend." Missy told nobody. The river's relentless rhythm echoed in her own heartbeat, a reminder that life's currents could be both thrilling and tumultuous. She resolved to unravel the mystery of Brandon's distance. Perhaps the Snake River held answers, its depths concealing secrets as ancient as the mountains guarded it.

Her journey from Nampa to Murphy, Idaho was a thirty plus minute drive southbound. In the quaint town, small enough to be mistaken for a ghost town, Missy found herself surrounded by rugged mountains, perfect for hiking and the river for fishing. She was away from home because an opportunity had arisen to join the Owyhee Gymnastics Team. Influenced by her parents' familiarity with the area and the comfort of knowing she would stay with a family they trusted, Missy hoped her gymnastics journey would be as remarkable as the rugged landscape that now surrounded her.

She settled into a spare bedroom at the house of her once best friend, Maura Derringer, but now they hardly stood each other. Julie Brown, her current bestie, had declared she'd lost her mind to move away from home and live with Maura. Maybe she had, but Missy needed a change.

After completing her first week of practice, the gymnastics team held a potluck in a park by the Snake River on Saturday, aiming to foster a close-knit community. Following lunch, while the team socialized, Missy sought solitude.

A catfish leaped out of the water, swiftly submerging again. *'A great place to fish.'* She glanced left and spotted a trail by the river, weaving through the trees. Curiosity overrode her common sense, and she stepped into the forest to explore.

She knew Starr Wilkinson, also known as Bigfoot, was buried in Owyhee County. Was she near his grave? After a minute of walking, no mythical creatures lurked behind trees or rocks. The trail veered left, leading to a small clearing with a manmade hut, a fireplace, and a stack of wood.

Despite her stomach tightening and an inner voice urging her to return to the picnic area, Missy couldn't resist snooping around to discover who might live there, perhaps a homeless person or someone seeking Starr's grave.

A laugh echoed, a female voice talking to another person. *'Great, it's Maura.'* Knowing Maura, she was talking to herself, or maybe an imaginary friend. No surprise if she was.

"Missy!" Maura called out.

Missy wanted to keep her discovery a secret and hurried back onto the trail. As she approached Maura, she heard a male voice questioning their presence in the woods.

"Why are we looking for Missy?"

"To ensure Bigfoot doesn't kidnap and tie her up in a cave," Maura replied.

Missy froze. No, Maura wasn't alone.

"Bigfoot?" the male voice asked.

"Brett, this is not the time for clarification. I'm not even sure I can make sense of Missy myself." Her tone was mixed with frustration and concern.

"How do you know her?"

"We grew up on opposite sides of the same neighborhood." Her voice softened, hinting at a history deeper than Missy had imagined.

"You recently moved to Murphy?"

"Yes. Didn't want to at first. I left my BFF who lived two houses down from me. But we rented the land for our horses. The owners moved to a warmer state and let us have the house."

"Interesting," Brett commented.

Missy met them by the river. Despite her urge to yell, "Shut up," she refrained to avoid giving Maura a sense of control.

"Ahh, there you are. It's time to come back. The coaches want to give closing remarks before we leave." Maura put her hands on her hips.

Missy waved to acknowledge she heard and would leave on her time, not her ex-friend's time. She kicked a big rock hard into the river. *This one's for you, Maura.*

A sparkle on the ground caught Missy's eye. She squatted to check it out. An arrowhead. She picked it up and stood. The last time she saw one was when the spirit of Chief Tso'ape-ha, John Badger, gave one to her younger brother, Tommy, by the irrigation ditch close to their home last year.

Missy's heart raced. Her priority was to uncover the truth, but above all else; face the currents of her life head-on, like the Snake River faced the boulders in its path. Caught up in her thoughts, she didn't hear the footsteps and shrieked as a hand touched her shoulder. She turned around, ready to fight.

"Whoa there." It was Reed Bell. He was the son of the head coach of the gymnastics team.

She put the arrowhead in her pocket.

"Are you okay? My dad's waiting for you."

"Yeah, fine. I'm ready to leave."

"Even though it's daytime, it's not safe to be alone," Reed warned.

She squinted her face in disbelief, though a strange feeling crept inside her skin. "Why not alone?"

"You need to believe me about not being alone."

"Fine. I won't." More like she would not follow his orders. Maybe he dealt drugs and the camping area was his hiding place.

They didn't talk during the short walk back to the park. She loved it here even more than the gymnastics her parents wanted her involved in. The mountains and rivers were her heaven, to be by herself and think clearly.

Upon arrival, Coach Bell restated the risk of being alone for extended periods near the river or in the woods. She sat by Echo Frame, who also seemed bored, and played a game on her cell phone through the motivational speech by both coaches.

"I hate 'make you feel good' talks," Echo whispered.

Missy nodded. When the time of boredom ended, Missy sprinted to her car. Aware of something forbidden lurking in or around Murphy, she devised a plan to unravel the unsettling mystery behind her nightmare's persistent presence.

Chapter 2

"Julie. Get over to my house now." Missy flopped onto her bed beside her duffle bag.

"You haven't been gone a week and miss me that much?"

"We need to talk. I'll see you on the trampoline."

"Yes, sergeant. Be there soon." Julie hung up.

Missy went into the kitchen and grabbed two water bottles out of the fridge. She turned and bumped into her mom.

"You entered your room without a greeting, scurrying like a frightened mouse."

"Sorry. I had to call Julie. We need girl talk." She held up the water. "Practice was simple. We went over the rules, safety, equipment, blah, blah, blah."

"Blah, blah, blah?" Her mom raised her eyebrows.

"Yeah. Nothing major. It was kinda boring." Missy took small steps toward the rear door. "I'll tell you more later." She didn't wait for a response and went outside, while Julie entered through the back gate.

The girls laughed as they jumped on the rectangular ground-level trampoline under an oak tree. Julie raised her arms and grabbed a handful of leaves on her way down. "I'm a bird."

"Flap your arms harder." Missy did a backflip. "You might fly home."

"Funny. Not. Still can't believe you followed Maura to Murphy for a gymnastics team. I thought you were excited they'd moved to another town."

"After Brandon dumped me, I had to leave and pursue my dreams."

"Poor Ms. Snobby, Ally Norcross, will miss her bestie, Ms. Attitude, Maura." Julie spun in a circle.

"I don't care. With Maura gone, I'm sure their neighbors noticed the calm. Those two together explode with attitude."

"True," Julie agreed.

"Weird thing—in our first week of practice, I had no problems with Maura." Missy crossed her fingers. "The stress of waking up early and working our butts off has kept the team mellow. Maura's big sister, Sandy, and little brother, Jake, are nice, but their 'Moom' is almost as nice as my mom." She did a seat drop to end the jumps.

Julie copied. "I don't understand why you call her Moom." She reached over and tickled Missy's feet.

"Hey, there." She bit her lower lip. "When Maura and I met in kindergarten, she talked to a lady I didn't recognize. I was eating a cookie, and it sounded like I asked, 'Is that your moom?' instead of mom. Maura's mom, Linda, thought it was cute and liked the new name."

"Surprised she never freaked out about it."

"Me too. But Maura also knows her mom likes me." She made an arrogant face.

"Why don't you call her dad, Craig, Daam?" Julie crunched the leaves in her hand.

"You could try it, like misspeaking, and fix it with Daad. Plus, I'd feel bad if I did, and to top it off, if Maura heard, she'd mouth off crap back to me." She picked up a stick and broke it.

"I sense the stick break is how you feel. About ready to snap."

"You read me like a book, Julie. I show no emotions, and you know."

"It's the way you broke the stick."

Missy rolled her eyes and broke another one. "Two negatives. One, living with Maura. Ally hitting on Brandon, and adding a third, leaving my friend," she pointed at Julie, "behind."

Julie smiled. "Back to your team. Will you come home every weekend?"

"The schedule fits me. On Monday mornings, I set foot in Nampa High's office, turn in my homework from the previous week, and pick up any assignments. We meet at the gym in Murphy every Monday at noon and practice until four. Tuesday through Friday, we practice from eight until noon, have a lunch break, and do schoolwork from one until four. On Saturday, we practice from nine until one unless we have a gymnastic meet. Afterward, I come home to spend time with my family and this cool person I've dealt with, minus Brandon."

Julie threw the crunched leaves at Missy. "Any cute guys in tight shirts showing off their muscles?"

Her cheeks heated. "Can you believe Maura is on the hunt? She's already preying on a team member named Brett. She's like a bear finding fresh meat. My focus lies in gymnastics, not relationships." Missy twisted her hair. "But."

Julie's eyes widened. "But what?"

She cleared her mind of missing Brandon. She didn't want a soap opera life. Besides, Missy knew she was too young to get serious at fifteen years old. "Everyone on the team is nice-looking."

Julie hesitated for a moment. "You're hiding something. I'm not worried though. You'll tell me soon. So, how many are on your team? Will you have a personal coach?"

"Sixteen. We're separating into groups of four tomorrow. Last week was off balance. All we really did was cover safety, the proper ways to stretch, and find the exact space between the high and low bars. The next step was to locate our spot on the runway for mounting the springboard for the vault. Pat Bell and Kirk Hopkins are the head coaches, and we have four assistant coaches."

"Interesting."

"You know how we thought Maura's name was odd?" Julie nodded.

Echo and Vallie Frame are the two sisters on the team. "Are you kidding me?"

"Nope." She raised her eyebrows.

"I see you've got more gossip to tell me. You're about to burst." Julie leaned forward.

Missy slapped her thigh. "Reed Bell, Pat's son, comes and helps when needed. Despite graduating early during his junior year, he had been a state champion in gymnastics for the last couple of years and is remarkable. He's seventeen."

"You think you're going to chase him?"

"No way. There are prettier girls on the team than plain me. Anyway, Coach Pat wants us to be more of a family. At practice, we call them Coach Pat and Coach Hopkins. Kirk likes his last name better. But on Monday nights, when we have dinner at the Bells' house, it's Pat and Kirk. Confusing, if you ask me. Anyway, Pat lives a five-minute walk from Maura's."

"Still sounds interesting." Julie stood. "One more question. I remember last year you told me Bigfoot died in the Murphy area. Has your sixth sense tingled?"

"Hate to say it, but yes. Before I came home, I wandered off by the river and saw a camping area. It gave me the shivers. Our coaches cautioned us against spending too much time on secluded train tracks, trails, or the river."

"Why?"

"I don't know. It may be impossible to avoid a train when on the tracks. Wild animals will eat you. Maybe it's a homeless person's living area I saw. The caves may have additional hazards, making them unsafe."

"Looks like it's time for the Missy Mack Detective Service to investigate," Julie said.

"Missy Mack's only purpose is gymnastics."

"Sure. I'll die if I know you didn't go back and check it out." Julie laughed. "Time to finish my homework for Monday. See you next weekend." She bounced off the trampoline.

"See you later." It was Missy's turn to jump off. She had to finish a few English papers but thought she'd write in her journal first.

"If I had a degree in psychology, I'd still have difficulty figuring out your crazy mind." Julie shrugged, gave a single wave, turned, and shut the back gate.

***

September 19
Dear Diary,

Thank goodness for free time to type since my parents got a computer with a printer. Now my hand won't get cramps from writing. It's nice to not live in the Little House on the Prairie era. Well, almost. I would make the Guinness World Book of Records as the only sophomore without a cell phone.

Anyway, Julie believes I've lost my mind. Maybe I have. Even if I had a cell, the connection in Murphy is terrible and a desolate boring area except for the Snake River flowing, finding an arrowhead, and the manmade camp. Will there be more?

Pat gave us the rules. First is to be punctual, even when you're on your deathbed. I wonder how Maura will cope with that one.

Missy listened to Tommy complaining about his homework to their mom. *Poor little brother. Not. He's fortunate to have a computer for most of his upcoming school years with no hardships, unlike me.* Glancing at the printer, she confirmed the paper supply.

Oh, yeah, Pat added this.

'There are movie nights and dances with other nearby towns, like Melba. It's a break from the repetitive daily routines. We'll keep you posted.'

I hope some excitement happens soon because sitting around Maura's house watching TV or in my room doing nothing is boring.

She saved her entry on her USB, printed off her entry to put in her notebook, and made sure her journal wasn't auto-saved on the computer's hard drive, but not before thinking again of the Snake River and her run-in with Reed and the arrowhead.

Chapter 3

Missy's inner thigh muscles stretched during a warm-up side split. Despite being at the gym, she longed to be out hiking, fishing, or engaging in other activities. She switched to the Chinese split position, leaned forward, and laid her upper body on the floor between her legs. She knew the start of week two would be torture and contemplated her decision to be a gymnast.

Was this her dream, or merely the fantasy of her parents? Did she want this?

Echo tapped Missy's back. "You awake? Coach Pat called us to the side of the floor. Time to set up the groups."

She pulled her body forward and got up.

Maura, a magnet to gossip, passed by at the wrong time. "Yep. Missy holds the golden ticket for spacing out. Hmmm, I bet you're picking out a new guy to replace Bran—"

"Shut up." Missy was tired of Maura, who loved to walk all over her.

"Woo-hoo. Who stepped on your toes?" Maura's hand rested on her chest.

"You. Back off!" Missy gave her a death glare.

Maura's expression went from a fake shock to a real one. "Sheesh."

Oh, my gosh! Her jaw dropped in astonishment at Maura's look of defeat. She longed for the day when she would see Maura have a brief emotional meltdown.

Echo handed Missy her water bottle. "Time to put out the flames. I still see the steam above your head. Is she like this with you at her house?"

"I stay away from her at home if her family isn't close." She shrugged and drank half her bottle. Missy would not admit it scared her to death to voice her opinion to Maura. Her heart raced as she expected the daunting task of facing Miss Thinks She's Perfect after practice.

Echo shaped her mouth like a silent 'O.' "Here's some positive news to cool you off more. I saw Reed checking out how flexible you've become. Ooh, la la." She amplified the last comment.

Missy quivered. "I'm done with them." She spoke under her breath and tossed her bottle near her sweats, which were placed against the wall.

Coach Pat tapped his clipboard to draw attention, and Coach Hopkins cleared his throat. "I see you've finished your warm-ups. Make a line." He pointed to the side of the floor.

The team stood on the white border. "The first four on my right, find a spot on the floor." Hopkins pointed. Missy was number two and stood in the middle of the floor. "The next four in line, go stand by your number." Echo adjusted her position in line to end up in Missy's group. "Repeat for the last four."

Coach Pat took over. "You'll be with your group for the season." He wrote on his clipboard. "Group one is Vallie, Paul, Chris, and Matt, with Doug as your coach.

Group two is Missy, Echo, Tony, and Chad, with Kimberly as your coach. Group three is Maura, Staci, Brett, Leo, and Laura as your coach. Group four is Gwynn, Leslie, Rich, Dave, and Aaron as your coach." Coach Pat put the pen on the clipboard. "After two hours of practice, we will switch positions of where we put your number. Got it?"

All agreed.

"Each day will be different. If required, your group may work on the floor and bars for two consecutive days or solely on the beam all day. So do your best to move on."

Everyone went to their destination. A folding chair sat by each station with a number attached. Missy's team started on vault and the guys on the pommel horse.

When the first two hours ended, Missy remembered the junior high gymnastic team practices and labeled it a 'Practice for Preschool Kids.' If this was what gymnastics entailed, she was in for a painful journey ahead. The mountains beckoned to her, but when would she have the chance to return?

***

Missy dreaded the drive to her temporary home with the Derringers and prayed Maura wouldn't be waiting in her bedroom.

She was relieved to see only Linda inside. "Hi, Moom."

"How was practice?"

"Harder than last week, but it'll get better."

Moom nodded and went back to reading.

She stopped by Maura's closed bedroom door and heard her talking on the phone.

Maura recounted, "Missy bluntly told me to be quiet and stay out of her affairs." A brief pause. "She took her sweet old time getting off the floor stretching, and I asked her if she was tired. She threw a fit and yelled. I tried to cover for her as she drew unwanted attention. I'm sure she'll be off the team before our first competition."

Missy tightened her fists to stop the urge to pound on Maura's door. She controlled herself, went into her room, locked the bedroom door, and stared at her suitcase and duffle bag. It would be easy to fill them up and leave.

To prove to herself and the team she wasn't a wimp, she took a shower to wash off the sweat and negative attitude she had toward Maura.

The hot water sprayed on Missy's back, and she wished it was molten lava hitting Maura's perfect body. She couldn't believe her negative comments. The living situation at the Derringers had become tragic. She stuck her tongue out at the wall and imagined Maura's flawless face.

Her fingers throbbed as she scrubbed her head raw with the shampoo and conditioner. She finished her shower, got ready for the evening drama, opened her door a crack, and lay on the bed.

The light beige walls had only two flower pictures, offering little visual interest. She tried to make out objects on the ceiling spackle besides shapes of arrowheads and Indian chiefs, but it was no use. The mountains, the caves of discovery, everything she loved, had to wait. At least the team's dinner tonight at the coach Bell's house will be social and not practice. Maura knocked on Missy's bedroom door and jingled her keys. "You're more than welcome for a ride to the Bells' house. My muscles ache too much for a walk."

"Thanks." She got up, followed her to her car and was surprised Ms. Two-Faced Queen Maura admitted she had pain, let alone offered her a ride.

The short drive was silent. The Bells' front door was open, so they let themselves in. Missy saw Echo sitting with a plate of food. She pointed to an empty chair by her. Missy got the hint, but almost changed her mind to sit by the food instead as she loaded up her plate with shrimp, shrimp, and more shrimp. To balance the plate, she added cheese, crackers, and grapes.

Echo pushed the chair back to give room for Missy to sit. "Don't you love the variety of food?" She dipped a carrot into the ranch dressing on her plate.

"I'm in Heaven eating shrimp non-stop."

Coach Pat stood and welcomed them all. "A new week, a new beginning. Questions?"

Chris raised his hand. "My family moved to Melba last year and heard rumors about Bigfoot. What do you know?" A few team members giggled, and a fake cough came from Reed.

"Good question," answered Pat's wife, Chaundra.

"Can you get me a glass of water, please?" Coach Pat asked his wife. She brought out a tall glass of ice and a pitcher of water. He swallowed several times to water his mouth for a long story. "Around this area by the Snake River in 1882, a Native American had several names. He's known best as Chief Nampia or Bigfoot, but his real name was Starr Wilkinson."

Starr didn't settle well with Missy. Her stomach tightened, making her nauseous. Others in the room rolled their eyes in disbelief.

Pat continued, "I grew up not too far from this house. Between college semesters, I worked on the farm to buy an engagement ring for my beautiful wife. I also lived independently in the small guest house at the end of the field by the river." He sat on a chair by the table. "For years, I've had several dreams about history. I don't believe in reincarnation, but I think our inner spirits can briefly time travel to other bodies and past places. Back in 1882, working in the logging company, arrows from Native Americans shot the workers and me. One arrow hit my left lung. I fell and could barely breathe."

The coach asked if anyone knew about time traveling, then pointed to himself without waiting for an answer. "I went back in time to save myself and will share the details later." Pat looked at a picture of the Snake River above the fireplace.

Pat's beliefs didn't settle well with Missy. She felt perspiration on her forehead, left the room, and met Mrs. Bell in the kitchen. "Can I use the ladies' room?"

She gave Missy a half hug. "No need to ask and make yourself at home."

"Thanks." She wanted a break from hearing about ghosts and looked at the bathroom mirror as confusion blasted through her brain. Missy attracted this kind of attention everywhere she went. Starr, arrowheads, and Coach Bell stories. She washed her hands and looked one last time in the mirror before leaving. She gasped when words in red looked back at her.

GO HOME.

Missy rubbed her eyes, looked again, and the words were gone. She knew her imagination was active, but this had to be stress. The statement fueled her determination to explore the tracks and search for hidden caves. She returned to her seat in the dining room as Pat ended his story and wished she had stayed longer in the bathroom.

"Before I fell, I saw the three guys who shot Starr. Starr himself looked at me in his last minutes of life, held up a small object, and whispered, 'Why didn't you stop them?' and died. The fear and threat still haunt me." He watered his dry mouth to the last drop in his glass.

"Back to my youth as a worker living in the guest house. A couple of days went by, and I swear on the holy grave I saw a wild black dog or wolf come to my door, scratch on it, and howl. Common sense told me to put my scraps of meat and bones on a plate and set it out on the front porch. I didn't dare pet the dog for fear of being bitten."

Pat had everyone's attention. Missy glanced over at Reed and didn't doubt he'd heard the story countless times. He sensed her stare and returned it with a smile.

"One night when I was in bed, noises like a thief trying to break in woke me. I saw a fully dressed Native American Chief stand in my doorway. He turned to leave, and I followed. As I reached the door and glanced, he transformed back into a dog and fled." Pat stood. "Afterward, I moved back home. I didn't want to deal with it again."

A hand rose.

"Question, Rich?"

He cracked his knuckles. "Let me get this straight. You dreamed of getting killed, saving yourself and possibly Chief Bigfoot?"

"To an extreme, yes. You need to live through it to understand."

"So, you're saying dreams happen, or you're living in your dreams? Like it controls what you're doing?" Staci showed interest.

"Dreaming is dreaming, but feeling things in your dreams is real." Pat rubbed his forehead. "Enough for tonight."

Missy pondered as the team left for their cars to go home. She understood what Pat had said. Someone else's experience convinced her she wasn't going through the same thing alone.

Maura rambled on in the car and into her house. "Did you believe one word out of Pat's mouth? Oh, my gosh. It brought back memories of you seeing a ghost driving a tractor." Maura snickered. "And to claim that Bigfoot, or whoever the guy is, is haunting you again. Coach Pat has sniffed too much horse poo if you ask me." Maura walked to her room, shut the door, and continued to talk to herself.

The pressure at practice and the mental trauma during dinner weighed heavily on Missy, pushing her toward leaving. It scared her to use the bathroom in case another message appeared in the mirror. Fortunately, it shined clean and new.

Curious, Missy ventured to the back yard and followed the path to the river. She fought with herself not to cross over the bridge and have a ghostly creature throw out its tentacles and grab her.

She stepped closer to the river's edge, expecting a bright red message telling her to run for her life. The sound of a rock hitting the train track scared her. Missy looked over at the mountain curve and saw a dim light disappear.

Suddenly, her foot slipped on the muddy wet grass. She flapped her arms to break the fall and landed on the slanted edge. She tasted water as her face kissed the river.

And then it came. Did the mirror message point to Reed or his dad being involved in the dealing? Another thought crossed her mind. Starr's grave could be nearby, and she needed to find it before anyone else did.

Missy spit as she pushed herself up and wiped the debris off. "Clumsy, clumsy, klutz! Gosh flipping darn it. I'm not trying to drown myself." She approached the bridge's edge.

"Here I go." She made it across, stepped on the tracks and hoped to see whoever went around the corner. Missy got twenty yards on the track when she felt her feet vibrate. "Earthquake?"

The loud sound of the horn echoed from a freight train. In the absence of crossroads, she hoped the train had notified the person on the tracks. She hurriedly returned to the safe side of the bridge. Missy had no desire to witness the gruesome scene of blood, guts, and body parts scattered on the front of the train. She hoped the person had gotten off the tracks in time.

As she got ready for bed, her mind felt like a rollercoaster. *Did the person who killed Starr push him into the river? Or was he buried near the river?*

Oh, to sleep through the night. But as she closed her eyes, the nightmare started.

Restless in the evening, she explored an old shack in an empty field. "Time to solve Starr's mystery." Missy opened the shack's door.

"Enough to drive me crazy."

She recognized the voice and shuddered as it lingered in the air. Jim Forst was rocking back and forth as he sat in the chair. The shed had an open hole in the corner. "You'll get caught when the police find you." She stepped forward.

"Nah, I'm a ghost. I have the freedom to come and go as I please."

"What are you doing?" Missy asked.

"Awaiting Chief Starr's arrival from the tunnel."

"Why?"

"I worked out a deal to get a break from you. I'm letting Starr take over to give you nightmares, so I have time to make and sell my secret powder."

She froze, not knowing whether to run, scream, or go up and push Jim off the rocking chair. She chose the first as Chief Starr climbed up the ladder from the tunnel.

He smiled, laughed, and called out to Missy as she ran out the door. "I'll get you soon."

A charley horse jolted her awake. She stretched out her leg, grabbed her toes to pull her foot toward her knee, and massaged her left calf. To have Jim resurface in her mind only told her one thing. He was back in town. To picture her mom as Jim's girlfriend in high school made her sick. This was why she felt the connection. To stop all contact, she wanted him dead. He had no right to return to Idaho and mess with her. *How was Jim connected to Starr?*

She fluffed her pillow and tried to get comfortable before falling asleep.

Chapter 4

It was Tuesday, the middle of the night, and Jim Forst was coasting his 1977 Dodge Aspen down the Northside Highway exit ramp in Nampa, Idaho. The Sugar Factory sat one hundred yards from the exit and reeked seventy percent of the time with the smell of burned peanut butter. Jim rolled his window down to see how strong the scent was. "Only a faint smell tonight," he said.

Jim's partner in crime, Dwight Hartley, faked a laugh. "Interested in taking a strong factory whiff?"

"Any potent smell is better than your B.O. Since we passed Mountain Home, you've been sweating like a wet dog and stinking up my car," Jim complained.

"I'm a nervous wreck. We left on sour terms."

"We are hidden creatures, and nobody will ever find or remember us." A sliver of pain stabbed Jim's forehead. Time for another sniff of Twist.

"Ghosts. We're ghosts floating in the night."

Jim twitched. "Never, I seriously mean never, bring up that topic again. I've heard enough about ghosts." He continued the short five-minute drive to the older section of town.

Dwight okayed Jim's comment and stared out the window. "It looks like a gho-. I mean, the town looks empty in the middle of the night."

A streetlight flickered as Jim turned in the alley to park behind Jenkins' Antique Store. It was 2:00 a.m. "Does your daughter know we're here?" Jim eyed Dwight.

"Ruth will open the door soon." He sent another message to his daughter, who managed the antique store. Her living quarters were above the shop in the back area.

Ruth peeked out the back door. Her red hair looked like a mop as she scanned both directions of the alley and nodded the coast was clear. She pushed the door wide open. "Hurry! The shop down the street gets deliveries close to this time."

The men hurried inside Ruth's living area. "What sales trip are you on now?" She handed each a lunch bag with food.

"Thanks." Dwight peeked inside, smiled, and glanced at Jim.

Jim rubbed his eyes. "Portable storage compartments sound good?" He'd lied about his life for as long as he could remember. Jim's parents and grandparents had taught him to live freely and not get caught. They were the ones who introduced him to making, taking, and selling drugs.

Ruth folded her arms and rubbed the sides. "I can't keep hiding you two. You know that, right? It puts me at fault. I know what you're doing even though you haven't told me." She looked at her dad.

Dwight shrugged. "You aren't to blame."

Jim reiterated what he thought Dwight meant. "We have told you what we do. It isn't illegal to sell storage bins." Hoping Dwight got the hint, he left to get in his car. He did, with Ruth following behind. As he drove off, he saw Ruth's wave in his rearview mirror. Jim reached the end of the alley and heard sirens.

"They can't know about us yet." Jim's hands became clammy, and he turned onto a different street. He saw the flashing red and blue a couple of blocks from where he'd intended to drive.

Dwight tightened up. "The cops know nothing about us. They think stupid kids are causing trouble, I bet. Our connections in Murphy are waiting."

"Text them we ran into trouble and we'll see them later in the afternoon."

"Where are you going?" Dwight raised his voice in fear.

"Ever wonder what your Red Line Autos looks like now after you've been gone?" Jim rolled down the window again to inhale the cleaner, crisp fresh air. "I want to check out the shed by your office in the lot."

"Why?"

"It's a local place to hide and make Twist to avoid the police."

Dwight spaced out for a short time. "There's a tunnel entrance where we can do it, just not in the office or shed. I still have my brew there."

Jim slowed as he saw more flashing lights in the rearview mirror. "We are a nameless car driving through the night." Braking to a crawl, he expressed, "There's no excuse to pull me over." The police passed and turned in the opposite direction. "Talk about nightmares in Nampa." He continued to his destination.

Dwight, still tense, hesitated. "Why did you decide to return and open a shop? It's been less than a year."

Jim pulled into the Red Line Autos lot and parked by the shed. "I excel at hiding as a ghost." He looked around the car lot under the dim lights. "Still looks the same."

"You didn't want to hear the word ghost again, but now you're saying you're a ghost. You're not making sense."

Jim ignored his comment. They exited the car, grabbed flashlights, and descended the shed ladder into Dwight's forgotten lab. He found the light, turned it on, and circled in awe. "Why didn't you tell me about this when we first met?" His voice held a slight annoyance.

"I don't know. It's not mine. And for legal reasons, I did my best not to use it. The owner would threaten me if I did, or I'd pay for it."

Jim's eyes darted around, excitement building as he imagined money and drugs dancing in his mind. "What do you mean?"

Dwight searched through every drawer and cupboard, hoping to find something to sniff. "My math teacher in high school, Mr. Atkins, owned it. He was a big, bulky guy and high most of the time." He picked up a tiny pile of green dust, sniffed it, and dropped it on the ground. "I needed extra income and helped him out after school, on weekends, and during the summer." Dwight messed around with the drug machine. "I stayed in the office ninety percent of the time while Mr. Atkins made, sold, and took drugs." He strolled around the small underground room. "After graduation, I took over as Mr. Atkins retired early and left, I believe, before he got caught selling drugs to kids at school. Last I heard, he's in Seattle."

Jim held a big smile. "Can't you smell it? Can't you smell the new drugs and the piles and piles of money?"

"Yes, I can," Dwight said. "Yes, I can."

Jim and Dwight slept on the floor in the shed for fear of getting caught in the car. It wasn't a pleasant place to sleep.

Jim rolled over on the hard ground. "My body feels like it got run over by a tractor," he groaned and situated his jacket as a replacement for a pillow. "Let's purchase sleeping bags and other necessities for living in Murphy's cave and Nampa's tunnel."

"Kuna has a sports store. We can hit it on our way to Murphy." Dwight lay on his back and stretched out his arms and legs. The scent of earth and aged wood brought solace.

Jim continued to groan as he fell asleep, but it didn't last long. Suddenly, his cell's vibration echoed as it bounced on the floor. He looked at the screen. "What the heck? Why the blazing burgers is Rock texting me in the early morning?"

Dwight sat up. "What does he say?"

"They'll be at the BF Café in Murphy at eleven a.m. He'll guide us to where we need to park. Then we'll hike behind him to the cave."

"How did you get acquainted with Rock's Edge, anyway?"

"The sniffing Twist makes you forgetful. I went to school with Rock's brother, Steve. Interestingly, Steve is a pastor while Roger, also known as Rock, for Rock's Edge, leads a drug gang in Caldwell."

"The good and the bad. So, why are we using the cave in Murphy?"

Jim scratched his head. "I won't repeat myself."

Dwight was silent.

"Rock's Edge found a discreet place by Caldwell. He's also passing off dealers to us in Murphy's neck of the woods. See why we came back? More opportunities than in Arizona making and selling drugs."

"Don't worry. I won't ask again." Dwight lay back on the hard dirt floor. In only seconds, Jim heard him snoring.

Yes, they would make tons of money, and Dwight—forgetful and empty-headed Dwight—would help him do it.

Chapter 5

Jim kicked Dwight's butt and pushed him over. "Wake up, old goon, and step on it. It's nine o'clock." The smell of his partner in crime made him want to puke. "And after the meeting, I'm tossing you into the river. You stink to high heaven and back."

Dwight opened his eyes a sliver and scowled. "At least I didn't keep you up all night passing putrid farts." He stood and stepped out the door. "I'll be ready to leave after using the bathroom in the office."

Jim followed. He heard Dwight dropping things to the ground as he took a sponge bath.

On the way to Murphy, they grabbed a bite at Red Steer. "Our first stop is at a gymnastics gym. The new dealer works there. His name's Reed. He's in on the meeting with Rock." Jim tossed half his breakfast sandwich out the window into a cornfield. "Worst crap I've eaten. Dirt would've tasted better." He swallowed soda through the straw.

"It's the dirt you swallowed breathing with your mouth open as you snored all night." Dwight dipped a tater tot in the cup of fry sauce. "Tastes good to me."

Jim arrived ten minutes later and parked at Owyhee Country Gymnastics. "Stay put. I'll be back with Reed."

Jim exited the car, shot Dwight a deadly glare, and headed into the gym.

Reed came out of the office and met Jim in the observation room. "Good morning."

Jim nodded. "Ready to do some dirty work?"

"Can't at the moment. Got new team members, and it's my responsibility to train them well before the first meet."

"You wimping out on me?"

"No, sir. You can count on me. I have connections." He moved his head a bit toward the gym.

Jim raised his hand, left, and felt his life in Murphy was trouble-free with his side helpers. Reed went back into the office.

Jim got back into the car. "Reed can't make it. A new team needs help prior to the competition.

"You sure he isn't pooping out?"

"Yes." Jim backed out of the parking lot. "To tell you the truth, I only want us in the cave. Reed might have a slip of the tongue and blow our hideout by accident." He went on and complained about nothing going his way smoothly until he pulled into the BF Café. He saw his nightmare and felt worse by the smell of Dwight. "Not the person I want to see."

"Is he the big guy from New Mexico?"

"Yes. Carlos gives me the quivers."

Jim and Dwight exited the car, and Jim broke the silence. "Hey, there, Carlos, Rock. What gives? Where's your gang members?"

Carlos's pat on Jim's back was more like a warning. "They had other obligations, and I was in town to substitute."

"What gives?"

"I received news about a new shop closer to my people. I've been in the cave for years and thought it would be best for you, Jim. The cave has its perks, along with ghosts, but nothing to worry about," Carlos smirked.

Dwight giggled like a girl, and Jim elbowed his gut hard to shut him up. "We also have a backup option available, if needed."

Carlos and Rock raised their brows.

Dwight coughed. "A tunnel in my car lot. The entrance is in a shed fifty feet from the office that my old boss set up."

Carlos smiled. "Mr. Atkins. A good man. Passed away a short time ago." He nodded to Rock, showing it was time to go to the cave.

The desert landscape flashed by until Jim slowed down to turn. He followed Carlos up a narrow dirt road to a small spot to park. There was a trail leading to the train track.

Rock reassured Jim and Dwight they were safe. Jim was hesitant about the location because he saw several hiking trails close to the cave. Jim decided he enjoyed having a backup plan at Red Line Auto's secret tunnel.

They arrived at the cave three minutes later, walked through a narrow entrance a few yards away, and entered an open area with machines, generators, and drugs. Following a brief tour, Rock departed.

"What are your thoughts?" Jim surveyed the area. He was excited about Rock's set-up in the underground lab with electricity connected to the main tunnel leading to the train depot in Nampa.

"Besides crossing my fingers so I don't get claustrophobic, we've hit the jackpot." Dwight rubbed his hands together.

Buried Secrets

On their way back to Nampa, Jim and Dwight made quick stops in Kuna to grab camping gear from the outdoor store and food from the grocery store. They found refuge in their homemade bedroom, tucked away in a hidden corner of the tunnel, hoping for privacy.

Chapter 6

Mrs. Derringer got up early to make a breakfast of eggs, fruit, and croissants.

"Coach Pat expects us to be perfectionists in two weeks and add to our routines." Maura frowned.

Missy waited for her to continue her saga from last night about the coach sniffing horse poo. She didn't. "Thank you for breakfast, Moom. It was yummy."

"You're welcome." She turned to her daughter. "Why the grumpy look?"

"I'm not used to waking up early." She and Missy picked up their duffle bags. "I'll drive."

They'd agreed to take turns driving each week. This week was Missy's turn, but she knew Maura was a control freak and flaunted her brown Buick LaCrosse CXS. Yes, it was a nice car, and she didn't mind using Maura's gas. It was the only nice thing Maura had ever done for her.

As they got out of the car after Maura parked, she made her usual sarcastic comment. "Are you close friends with Echo because you can hear her comments echo around a few times so you don't forget what she says?"

Missy pushed the passenger door close to a slam. "Same reason you're friends with Ally. When you look down a trashy alley, you're looking in a mirror. You two connect perfectly." She stopped herself from biting her tongue and knew it was a rude comment. She also knew apologizing was a waste of time. Heck, Maura had mouthed off to her for years and never apologized.

Maura entered the gym without glancing back at Missy, which suited her just fine. Missy put her belongings in the cubbyhole and sat by Echo.

"Good morning, all," Coach Pat began. His voice was stern, like a marine sergeant's. "Today, Tony and Chad, you'll practice on the rings and pommel horse. Group one on bars and beam, and group two on the opposite. Groups three on the floor and vault, and group four opposite. There is no time to mess around."

Echo smiled. "I dislike the beam."

"You're smiling? It's my worst, and I hate it." Missy yawned.

"I consider it a challenge to grow and like or even love it."

"Nice to know. My choice is floor and vault and well, skip the other two."

"Yep."

Coach Kim got their attention by clicking her fingers. "We will do more stretches geared toward the muscles you use on the beam. You'll discover muscles you never knew you had, so get ready." She handed the team ankle weights. "Wrap these."

Missy pulled a disgusted look. "My arms are sore from pretending to swim on the floor yesterday, and now it'll feel like I'm lifting a piece of concrete."

"Smile. It's a muscle relaxant."

Missy ignored the comment. She looked around. Leo hadn't arrived, and the coaches had said nothing. She hoped he wasn't dead on the train tracks or hadn't gotten hit or drowned in the river.

The group lined up by the beam, using it as a pole for their workout. Coach Kim showed them simple moves, but Missy's calves strained. The beam was the most brutal. She worked on her backflip on the lower beam and was confident she wouldn't fall off the high beam. She completed her routine with one slightly off-balance but no fall.

A wide smile spread across Missy's face, relieved she was done with the beam. The bars she could handle. Coach Kim adjusted the bars' distance to fit Missy's height. "Let's work on the Hecht mount."

Missy nodded, tightened her handguards, and dipped her hands into the bag of powdered chalk. *Okay, I got this.*

She ran four steps to the springboard. As she pushed off the low bar, a movement caught her attention in the observation room. It was her nightmare, Jim Forst, talking to Reed. She missed her high-bar grip and did a belly flop on the mat. It reminded her of the previous night by the river. Was her dream a premonition? Was Jim on the tracks? She caught her breath as Coach Kim and Echo ran to her side.

"Are you okay?" Echo rubbed Missy's back.

"I see the space between bars suits you fine. What caused you to miss?" Coach Kim helped her up.

She rubbed her eye. "I think a piece of dust got in my eye. I'm fine." She knew they both knew it was a lie, but it didn't matter.

"To me, it looked like you saw a ghost. You turned white." Echo walked with her back to the front of the bars.

"I'm fine. I'll concentrate better next time." She tried to redirect her mind to the bars and completed without a fall.

Missy had a light lunch and left early to study alone. Knowing the student aides would inspect the desktop history, she couldn't resist her curiosity about Murphy. Google listed recent train accidents and deaths. Thank goodness Leo didn't appear on the list.

She deleted the page and typed Starr Wilkinson. The same information she and Brandon had researched at the Nampa Library last year resurfaced. She re-read Starr's last day of life and the general location of his death. The killers might have buried him where he was killed. She didn't feel it was close behind the Derringers' but was confused about why she had received the messages. Maybe it was to caution her she'd run into Jim. Pat, as she knew had no connection to Jim, but did with Starr, whom Missy was eager to comprehend.

Missy's fingers jammed the keyboard when someone's hands touched the back of her chair.

"What are you looking at?" Maura asked.

Her mouse clicked the X to close the page, and she glanced behind her. "Setting up a personal email for school."

Maura nodded and moved across the room to sit next to Brett.

Close call. And she hadn't lied. She knew she needed to get a personal email besides the school's webpage to communicate with the teachers. Even with no computer, she could email Julie when she had access to one.

Missy's plan to find the program halted. The team entered the room for school. Pretending to do homework, she wrote the last year of her encounters with Jim, her new connections with Reed, Pat, and the camping area.

Should she tell Brandon she'd seen Jim? Or tell Brandon's dad, Dean Miller, who was on Jim's case in

Nampa? She thought of calling, meeting him, or showing up at the police station. But what if she'd only hallucinated? No. It was Jim, and her gut feeling of Reed being different was true.

Chapter 7

The Bell family sat leisurely at the kitchen table as Reed ate his dinner when, out of the blue, Pat commented, "I see you like a certain teammate."

Reed stopped chewing and spit out the piece of meat onto his plate. "It's natural for a female to add spark to your life."

Pat laughed. Chaundra shook her head. "She has the spunk to accomplish what she wants."

"I sense she's looking for something besides a gold medal."

"Like what?" Pat scooted forward in his chair.

"During your story about Starr, Missy left the room and looked scared." Chaundra wiped her mouth with a napkin. "She requested to use the bathroom, hinting at motives beyond a mere need. Would Starr have any connections with her?"

"Got me." Reed forked an uneaten piece of meat.

"See if you can find out. She can provide an extra perspective on hikes, helping you notice things you might miss.

"You mean you want me," he pointed to himself, "to drag Missy into helping me find the buried boxes and a cave of druggies? What if we run into Jim and his partner? They might cause her trouble."

"I agree with Reed, Pat. Running into drug dealers isn't safe." Chaundra pressed her lips together.

"I believe Jim doesn't want me to know where his cave is, so I need to find it. Having a partner to hike with might help."

Chaundra patted Reed's arm as she cleared the table. "If any information is in the box, it's all I have for any family connection."

"I'll do my best."

With the table cleared and leftovers in the fridge, Chaundra excused herself to her craft room. Pat motioned Reed to follow him outside onto their deck.

"Playing a drug dealer for Jim may seem simple, but his dangerous connections can escalate the situation. Although I dislike putting you in this situation, it's necessary to gather all the information. We lack sufficient evidence to apprehend Jim and the drug manufacturers. Plus, if the police department finds out our dear friend Sheriff Getter is letting an innocent minor citizen help him find the bad guys, we'll all be in trouble."

"I get it, Dad, but it's not abnormal for me to go hiking. This area is Heaven for hiking to countless people."

"However, people do not venture off the trail in search of dangerous places."

Reed raised his hands. "I'll be safe with or without Missy hiking with me. And I won't take her to unsafe places."

"I can count on you. Don't want my top gymnast getting hurt." Pat leaned forward and rested his hands on the rail. "And for your information, there are two teammates who use drugs. David and Leo. I don't want you to pay special attention to them."

Reed scratched the side of his head. "I get it."

Pat nodded his head in agreement. "David and Leo will remain silent, as they know you could report them. Jim's return prompts a meeting with the two of them, followed by your involvement. It's the game." Pat straightened from his lean. "Will you check out the other cave?"

"It's a short distance from the first one after the mountain point." Reed stepped toward the stairs at the end of the deck.

"Be careful." Pat touched Reed's back as he went inside. Reed flapped his arm once and continued his walk to the train track.

Chapter 8

Missy ate little during dinner and didn't join in the conversation with the Derringers. She helped Mrs. Derringer clear the table and excused herself for fresh air. The bright stars sparkled in the sky and made Missy want to walk. She crossed over the bridge and continued her journey on the train track. She needed a flashlight for the next trip in case there was a cave.

Nothing eventful happened, and she enjoyed getting away from the stress that was a part of gymnastics.

The place had an eerie vibe, reminding her of walking in the Nampa underground tunnel with Brandon last year.

She reached the mountain curve and paused briefly, listening for any sounds. Nothing. She shook her hands and continued around the curve.

What a relief. The surroundings resembled those behind the Derringers', except for the absence of flat land alongside the track. The right side led straight down to the Snake River, while the left had a steep five-foot drop. Descending would be simple, but ascending could be challenging.

She hadn't run into a wild animal yet or a dead body. She walked a few more steps and saw a cave opening. Without a flashlight, she needed to remember where to slide down the tracks and enter the cave. Perhaps other caves were close by.

Missy walked another minute and noticed a flickering light up ahead. Someone was close, and she wasn't ready to run into anyone. Quickly, her mind developed a plan. Perhaps a push into the water in self-defense would work. She regretted going out in the dark and resolved to plan her outings more carefully.

She sat on the side and slid downward. Pebbles, dirt, and weeds scraped her butt as she scrambled behind a large rock. She prayed the person didn't see her.

As the footsteps got closer, she squatted in a ball for double security, and her heart chugged like a tractor. The person stopped and panned a beam of light over her hiding place. She held her breath. It wasn't a flashlight. It looked like they were fiddling with a cell phone. "I thought I saw movement," someone said. "Probably a deer. The coast is clear." He directed the light on the track and walked around the point.

Missy shivered. It was Reed's voice. Was he the drug dealer helping Jim? She hoped Leo was sick or Reed was looking for him, too. She didn't know what to believe. It made her feel sick, and she didn't dare leave her hiding place. What if they were waiting around the bend, not wanting her to know they'd seen her?

Her heart continued to pound. Sometime later, Missy slowly straightened to a stand to make sure she was alone. Everything was fine until she turned the corner and noticed a dark figure on the tracks. Missy froze and prayed to heaven it was Reed. She lacked the ability to run without tripping on the tracks.

"Missy, is that you? It's Reed." She stood still as he walked back to her. "Why are you here in the dark? Don't you remember what my dad said?"

His comment provoked her. "I can ask you the same question." Ignoring what occurred; she hurriedly passed Reed on the tracks, rushed to the bridge, and sprinted to her room, seeking solace beneath the blanket.

***

Saturday morning, Missy loaded her car with her belongings to head home after practice. Since Tuesday, she'd kept low and had done her best to avoid Reed. The daily routines were brutal, and by the time she flopped on her bed at the Derringers', she was dead tired. Leo returned to the gym after being absent, and it relieved Missy that he wasn't dead.

The team met on the floor for closing remarks from Coach Bell. "Are the workouts getting easier for you?"

With the always cheerful smile, Echo touched Missy's arm.

"Four hours of practice feels like twelve," Missy said. She wanted to leave before she exploded.

"I get you. After two weeks, it gets easier. Want to hang out after the coaches dismiss us? We can either go to the BF Café for food or take a walk by the Snake near my house. It's beautiful."

"Thanks, but no thanks." Missy resisted the temptation to go to the river, considering last night's events. It was better to stay put. The untouched homework still awaited attention. "I'm not feeling up to par and want to go home."

Echo's eyes clouded over in sadness. "I'm sorry. I hope you feel better. My body isn't used to the hard work, either."

Coach Kirk raised his voice to draw attention. "Good news. The schoolroom is now optional. If you fall behind, we will know. If you are flunking classes, you'll be off the team. T.A.s will be available to help. You're dismissed, and have a great weekend. See you Monday."

The first person to leave the gym was Missy. She needed a break from Murphy, but her wish didn't happen easily. An auto accident on Highway 45 closed the road to add to the stress. During the hour wait, she thought of how to ask her dad for a laptop. She knew he'd come up with an excuse not to get her one. Informing him about the gym closure and homework might be the solution.

She parked her car in the driveway at home with her plan set. She entered the laundry room through the garage and dumped her clothes in the washer. The TV had a football game playing. Perfect. Her dad's focus on the game might make her speech a touchdown.

"Hi, Mom, Dad." She sat by her dad on the couch. "Miss me?" She hugged him. "Where's Mom?"

"In the basement with Tommy."

"So, um, I could use a laptop for school to make it easier to do homework."

A foul play distracted him. "Did you see that fumble?" He turned to look at his daughter. "And what is it you need?"

She expressed a sweet smile. "A laptop. Nothing fancy, only the basics with Word and Excel." She expected him to firmly address the negative consequences of the internet. She was wrong.

Her dad looked at his watch. "If we leave now and go to ABI, the owner, Mark Sweet, will give us a good deal." He stood.

"Are you serious?"

He patted her back. "I'm serious."

On the drive to ABI, Missy's dad had a boatload of questions to ask her about gymnastics. It made her head crazy. Why couldn't he ask her about her visits to the mountains or something important?

She did her best to tell him about her aches and pains of gymnastics, not including the stuff that needed to remain secret, hoping he'd stop asking questions.

"I'm proud of you. Life offers more than just desiring a cell phone and owning a computer. Mom and I were hoping gymnastics was the ticket."

Missy was silent; she tried to think of the new computer she'd be getting. It brought back memories of the excitement she felt as a little girl, picking out her favorite doll at the toy store.

"Thanks, Dad. You're the best," she said as they stopped in the parking lot.

He patted her back as they entered the store.

Mark smiled and greeted them. "Hello to my two favorite people. What can I do for you today?"

"My daughter needs a laptop for school."

"Follow me. We have a nice selection to choose from, including PCs and Macs. My preference is a PC."

Both examined various brands while Missy played with a few until she found a green one. "I'll take this one," she said, after hearing the sales pitch.

"Good choice."

Her dad purchased the laptop and made one last important stop. He treated Missy to her favorite, a peanut parfait at Dairy King.

"Thank you a thousand times, Dad. This will ease my schoolwork.

"The peanut parfait?" He laughed.

"Silly Dad. You know what I mean."

"If you need any help, come and get me or your mom."

"I will."

At home, Missy waited as her dad opened the front door. She sped to her room, put the laptop on her desk, and pinched her thighs to make sure she wasn't having a dream. The feel of the pinch and the red marks from her fingers proved she wasn't.

"Julie's going to faint," Missy said to no one in particular. She collapsed on her bed and dialed on the phone.

"I'm in Heaven," she said after the hello.

"Because you're talking to me?" Julie giggled.

"Close, well, partly. I'm lying on my bed and it feels like Heaven. Nice and soft. Want to come and see me? I've got a surprise."

"For me?"

"Not you, me."

"I'll be over soon." Julie hung up, was over in less than five minutes, and plunked down beside Missy.

"You were already skinny, but you look slimmer and firmer," Julie said.

"Thanks. Did you miss me?"

"I cried every night."

"Ha. I'm just happy I'm not by Maura twenty-four-seven. She caught her fish, and now she's hanging out with Brett."

Julie laughed. "Not surprised. You're still not interested in anyone?"

"I'm not interested in anybody on the team. I left Nampa to avoid relationships. Remember?"

"I don't believe you. Tell me."

"Nothing to tell." She thought Reed was hot but didn't want to chase him. She also couldn't tell Julie she'd seen Reed talking to Jim, at least not yet.

"Whatever." Julie pouted.

"Notice anything?"

Julie looked around Missy's room. "No."

"Silly goose, look at my desk." Her smile was big enough to cover her face.

"Oh, my heck. You got a laptop! No way. How'd you get it?" She sat on the chair to look at it.

"I asked."

"That's it?"

Missy nodded. "I need assistance with setting up an email address. What is the recommended option?"

"No problem."

A few minutes later, Julie helped her create a username she liked for social media. Instant messages came an hour later.

She continued telling Julie about the team and her coach. "My coach, Kim, is nice but a pusher. She made me practice the backflip on the beam until I could do it ten times with no fall."

"I'm impressed. Good job. More gossip news?"

"Thanks, on the flip. Maura has never mentioned Ally and Brandon at all. Speaking of Brandon. Do you see him much at school?"

"No more than normal. Brandon asked me during lunch on Wednesday if it was true about your plans." Julie leaned back against the wall. "I told him what I knew, and I hadn't talked to you since Monday. He thanked me for the information and left."

"Surprised he asked."

"Hit the mall or a movie?"

"Hard to believe, but I want to vegetate at home and mess with my laptop, but thanks."

"Ha, you don't want to see Brandon. Scared to cruise around on your motorcycle hoping he's out playing hacky sack with Kaleb?" Julie nodded and pointed her finger at Missy.

"There you go again, reading me like a book," Missy admitted.

"Friends are there to talk, but you're acting like a scaredy-cat."

"Can I share something without being judged?" Missy was used to Maura spreading any story with fault over detailed rumors.

"You can trust me."

Missy nodded. "Pat has dreams like my nightmares."

"About what?"

"Starr."

"Wow."

"No kidding." Missy continued to fill Julie in on Coach Pat's beliefs.

"You sure you don't need a break at the mall?"

"Nope. I want to veg on my very own bed."

Julie stood to leave. "Got horse duty to attack, so I'll see you later, gator.

"After a while, crocodile." Missy cleaned, organized her room, and stacked up a pile of clothes and a few odds and ends to donate to the local thrift store. In her spare time, she searched the internet for recent history about Starr and found a thought-provoking paragraph she didn't remember reading.

After Starr killed the lady he loved on the train, he married someone else and had a son. Over time, he became disconnected from both individuals. Perhaps Chaundra was a descendant of Starr's son and not the lady on the train.

On Google Maps, Missy saw several trails around the Snake River and the mountains. She knew there were bright headband flashlights in the camping bin in the garage to add to her duffle bag. She planned to see how Coach Bell's dreams combined with her dreams and figured hiking was a natural way to firm her leg muscles. *The dark caves will now be visible to me.* She chuckled, knowing she might find danger or deep trouble.

How could she fit in the search after practice without Maura asking questions? She searched in the camping bin. Her fishing pole, by luck, kept falling in her way. *Yes! This is it!* She grabbed her tackle box, net, and rod. Having her fishing pole and tackle box in the car would work. It would cover her tracks.

Chapter 9

Missy was determined to dig up clues and solve the long mystery of haunted secrets. Because of the shortness of time between practice and the Bells' dinner on Monday, she drove to the local convenience store on Tuesday evening.

"Can I help you?" a skinny, middle-aged lady with blonde hair asked. The name tag read: Jacquie.

"Hi, and sure. I'd like a map of local trails to hike on. You got one?"

"Of course. You look like one of the local gymnasts and a pretty one." She guided her to the other end of the store. "I don't understand why they opened a team here when we have close to zero population, but what can I say? People emerge from the ground to join."

Her understanding was remarkably accurate. *Ghosts are resurfacing.*

"Here's the maps. If you have questions, ask away." She pointed to her tag and returned to the store's front.

Missy browsed the maps and found an easy one to follow. On the other side of the river, trails were scattered, along with a train track behind the Derringer and Bells' houses, and more nearby, just a short drive away. She knew Starr and his grave might be a short walk away. What if she found it? Would she be cursed and struck by lightning?

She added a couple of candy bars and a water bottle to her purchases and left.

First on her list was to finish the next couple of days of school assignments in order to have Thursday free. Now, however, she needed an excuse to leave practice early. She crossed her fingers that she wouldn't get drilled by Maura.

Unfortunately, after Missy got home, Maura attacked her like a lion after raw meat. Without a greeting, she reached out to grab her bag and said, "Show me what you've got."

Missy pulled it back. "There's nothing important in here. Just a water bottle and some candy bars." The map was her secret.

"Boring."

Missy settled herself at the desk in her room and opened the algebra book. Wanting to tackle the toughest assignments first, she, not being the best at math, began her homework. She crossed her fingers. The five pages due by Friday wouldn't take much time. Thursday was her escape day.

Each day after practice, Missy worked hard to finish her homework, but Thursday morning hit her hard. She hated lying, especially if she got caught, hurt, or kidnapped for real by a lost soul in the mountains. A legitimate excuse for her absence was a hard task.

***

She pretended her reflection in the bathroom mirror was Maura.

"You see, I have a feeling I want to drive by myself. I'm not feeling very good."

"I know you want more 'me' time with Brett, so why don't I drive, and he can give you a ride home?"

Fetch. Both excuses sounded fake. She'd go for the second.

She entered the kitchen and grabbed breakfast. Maura wasn't present, only her mom.

"Good morning. You're up earlier than normal."

"Woke up full of energy." *Bonus for me.* "And ready to hit the day hard. I want to arrive before practice to work on my floor routine. I'm having a tough time getting it right."

Moom rested her hand on Missy's arm. "I'm so proud of you and Maura for your dedication. I'd rather be in a horse competition jumping fences."

"Can you tell Maura sorry for leaving her behind?"

"I will. But don't push yourself too hard. I'd rather not take you to the hospital and inform your parents."

"I'll be fine."

Missy finished her orange juice, grabbed a bagel to eat on the way to the gym, and wondered again about her idea.

After parking, she entered the gym, shoved her belongings into a cubby, and entered the bathroom. *I have mixed knowledge about what I'm doing. Gosh, darn it.*

She splashed cold water on her face to help her wake up and massaged her neck.

"Here goes the drama." She left the bathroom and walked quickly to warm up. Echo and Vallie were already there.

"Hi. Glad I'm not the only one early."

Echo waved. "Fifteen minutes isn't early."

The silence was broken by a door slamming in the workout area. Maura strutted over, and Missy was ready for a fight. "Early to work on your floor run? Can anyone accomplish anything in only fifteen minutes?"

"Every second without you feels like a miracle." Her gut clenched.

"Why am I nice to you when you are so rude back? You've got brain problems." She turned and met her group who had arrived for warm-up.

Echo tilted her head as if clueless about what happened. Missy shrugged back and finished her morning stretches.

Her first area was on the bars, and she did average in the workout. Next was the floor. Her stomach cramped, and it interfered with her routine. She came close to landing on her knees on the first run. She did her best to act sick and cover her story to Maura, hoping to leave early.

Coach Kim noticed and approached her. "Feeling, okay? You look pale."

Bingo. "Under the weather. It's uneasiness for the first competition, and my ankle is tender. I have a bone spur that acts up if I overuse it."

"Let's look." She led Missy to the medical section and had her sit on the bench. Kim moved her fingers around her left ankle. She put pressure under the ankle bone on the outside. "Where does it hurt?"

"Ouch. There."

Coach Kim wrapped an ACE bandage around her foot and ankle. "Stand up."

She stood. "I can feel the difference. Thank you."

"Head home, alternate ice and heat every twenty minutes, and take the day off. We'll check it tomorrow to see if it's okay for practice and the meet."

"I'm sure it will be, but resting now sounds like the healing miracle." She left with a fake noticeable limp.

The house was empty when she ran to her room to change her clothes. She skipped to the kitchen, grabbed bottled water from the fridge, and headed to her car. She hesitated to examine the map in the driveway, fearing Mrs. Derringer's arrival and questioning her well-being. Missy bit her lip and took the chance anyway.

Ten miles south showed an area of easy trails, and she doubted there'd be a grave there, but perhaps an excellent place to see if there were any clues or sixth-sense feeling.

The drive was short, and parking was right off the main road. A bridge over the Snake River led to five original trails. Some trails curved near the bottom of the mountains, and others reached the top. Missy chose the lower.

As she hiked, the sound of water from the river soothed her, and she loved it. The trail was well-traveled, but she knew valuable items were hidden in public areas. She saw a deer path up the side and followed it.

The trail started off easy but quickly became steeper. An enormous boulder made the deer path go around, but Missy saw indents for her feet to step in for an easy ten-foot climb. On the top was room for a couple tall trees for a perfect spot to sit and lean back on, and she set it as her turnaround point.

The fresh air and the sounds of the birds relaxed her. She wished Mother Nature could answer her questions and guide her to the destination she was looking for. A couple of hawks flew by. *Do they want me to follow them?*

With closed eyes, she contemplated her connection to Jim and his sudden reappearance. Then she remembered the warning note on the mirror in the Bells' bathroom.

Was the writer of that message scared she'd get hurt or discover something terrible and turn her in?

Please tell me. Please.

A wildcat ran in front of Missy and bounded up an unused trail. The cat made her notice a log sticking out of the ground. She walked toward it, ducking under a low tree branch.

The wildcat had vanished, yet she followed another constructed trail up the small hill. A cross, three feet tall, adorned the flat area on the top of the larger mountain.

By the call of nature, Sky Frame reached his place in Heaven.

Missy guessed Starr was the reason for Sky's death. *Dare I ask Echo about her brother?*

She walked to the side of the mountain near the cross, searching for an opening. *What if Sky worked on opening an entrance to the cave or built his own, and Starr had put a curse on him?* She saw a few pipe-sized holes someone had made.

Missy placed her hands on either side of her head and pushed hard. It was too much to figure out. An odd fragrance wafted from the holes. Not a bad smell, but different. She felt faint, sat, and closed her eyes.

***

A crunching noise woke Missy up. She saw three chipmunks playing in the leaves and climb up the nearby tree. The air seemed chillier, and the sun had moved to the west.

Did I pass out? Perplexed, she surveyed her surroundings and recognized the tree where she had first seen the wildcat. *What happened?* She trembled, certain she sat near the cave and someone had discovered her and brought her down the trail. She needed to leave.

Scrambling down the boulder, her foot stepped on a small rock, causing her bad ankle to twist. A sharp pain electrified her tendons. "Son of a gun. Ouch, ouch, and ouch!" She huffed and felt cursed because she'd lied about her ankle. This had to be the payback. The throbbing eased a minute or two later so she could walk.

By the bridge at the river, Missy sat down and took off her shoe, sock, and ACE wrap to soak her foot. When it turned red and went numb, she pulled it out of the water. A flash in the river caught her attention. There was another message.

You're in danger.

She stared back at an imaginary face. "No crap. If you're Chief Tso'ape-ha, can't you be more specific? Argh!" Not caring about the rocks or the sharp goat-head weed pocked in her arch, she jogged to her car and sat on the hood. She pulled the sticker out, quickly wrapped the bandage, and put her sock and shoe back on. Glancing back at her escape route, Missy wished the location was a mere illusion.

She sped to her temporary home and parked by Maura's car. It was 4:30 p.m. She expected a deadly gaze as she stepped inside the house. Maura sat by the computer table and looked ready to burst with questions, but kept her mouth shut. Missy held her breath until she'd settled in her room. She didn't get a visit from Maura. She sent a PM to Julie.

Missy: I can't hold a secret. Jim's back and I saw him talking to Reed. I'm going to get information from Reed about Jim and Twist. That's all I can say.

Julie: You're losing it. R U sure you're not hallucinating?

Missy: I'm not blind. Plus—never mind. I don't have time to explain.

Taking a deep breath, she tossed her phone on the bed, reminiscing about the crazy experiences no one would believe. Still, Julie was different, wasn't she?

Chapter 10

Reed parked by the rusted shed at the run down Red Lion Autos dealership. Dust covered the cars, and he saw that the local homeless had occupied some. Jim suggested using this place as the meeting base. Despite the cave in Murphy, Nampa remained the center point. Reed felt lost without knowing the location of Murphy's cave. He could point out several cave locations but was not surprised there were more. Curiosity piqued as he questioned their secrecy about the site, suspecting more than just drugs for sale.

He noticed the shed's door open, let himself in, and climbed down the ladder, muttering, "There's a chance I can get in serious legal trouble." When he reached the bottom, he heard Jim's voice.

"Dwight, looks like our man's here."

Reed rubbed his hands together to cover his insecurity. "Hey, guys. How's it going?"

"How's it going?" Jim skipped around in a circle. "We got it all. Two locations, more dealers, and soon more supplies." He pointed his finger at Reed.

Dwight stepped up and patted Reed on the back. "Jim's right. Our path leads to a life of wealth. Come look."

Jim pushed his way in front of Dwight to lead the tour. "As you see, here is the main operation center with the machines. But we are using other areas in the tunnel for extra operations. Follow me." He entered the tunnel. The battery-operated lanterns flickering on the sides of the cave gave it a haunted feel.

"Here's our sleeping room."

Reed saw the cots and air mattresses.

Jim showed other small rooms. One housed a stinky camping-size porta potty. "Though we have to walk a way to use it, the smell stays away from our sleeping and working area."

"Like we needed detail." Dwight plugged his nose. "Despite the office having a bathroom, Jim is afraid of being chased by a boogie man in the car lot."

"Shut up, and let me finish the tour." He showed the area in the tunnel where they dug up some old mugs and silverware. "What are your thoughts?" Jim asked, as he concluded the tour.

Reed felt like puking. "Seems like you got it all organized." He followed the two druggies back to where they started.

Jim explained and showed Reed how the machine worked on drying the drugs.

"Where are you, lazy boys?" Carlos yelled as he entered the tunnel room.

Jim cracked his knuckles. "Been checking out all the tunnels. Pretty cool. One led to my old shack in the field I dug up, but I saw several homemade ones. Lots of hiding places I like."

Dwight smiled. "Yes, sir. It is full of room to hide. You might also discover old items to sell for extra money."

Reed stood by the entrance. Despite never meeting Carlos, he had heard warnings about his intimidating nature.

"Speaking of cash." Carlos handed Jim a bank envelope along with a note. "This is the address to Garden City, where you buy supplies. Our customers are picky and want quality Twist products. Feel free to do as you please with the remaining money. I know you're broke. Get this area running, then hit the cave in Murphy." He turned to leave but stopped. "How's our Owyhee area dealers doing?"

Jim extended his arm toward the tunnel where Reed stood. "Got a gymnast worker and two team members ready to make their first purchase."

Carlos approached Reed and shook his hand, saying, "That's what I like to hear. Nice to have younger people on board." He didn't give Reed a chance to speak, waved, and left.

"I guess we'll hit Garden City and do a get-go of setting up." Jim opened the envelope and counted the fifty-dollar bills. "Is this real or counterfeit?"

Dwight grabbed one to hold up to the dim light. "Looks legit to me, but I could be wrong."

"I agree on that part." He shoved the money into his front pocket. "Time for you to scuttle, Reed. We need to get back to work."

They departed without checking if Reed was following. He wasn't. Instead, he snooped around.

He passed the porta-potty, using his cell light to search for other rooms. Despite a few covered openings, Reed didn't want to waste time sorting through rocks. He left after twenty minutes of prying, but a prickling sensation lingered on the back of his neck. He couldn't see anything but had a sneaking suspicion that hidden secrets were buried nearby.

Chapter 11

Fridays were Missy's bad days compared to everyone's good days. As Maura drove, she nonchalantly summarized her absence driving to practice. "Nice cover yesterday."

"Cover?"

"You and Reed."

"What?"

"Once you left, Reed followed suit and never came back. He's cleaning the equipment when we're at school. Where did you meet? Is he a good kisser?"

Missy opened and closed her mouth twice, not knowing whether to shout or cuss her out. "I never saw Reed yesterday. I discovered a fishing spot by the river." She rubbed her nose. "And soaked my foot."

"Uh-huh. Yeah, sure. I get it. Secret relationship." Maura nodded.

"You believe any made-up crap you want. But for the record, it's not true."

At the gym parking spot, Missy hastily jumped out of the car before it fully stopped.

"Wait until I tell Ally," Maura snapped back.

"Go ahead. I don't give a horse's butt," she steamed and went to the floor mat in the gym to warm up.

Missy saw Echo, who headed over to her, but shook her head. *Not in the mood to chat.* Echo acknowledged and sat by her sister.

Before practice, Coach Kim checked Missy's ankle. "Looks like you're doing well," she said, passing her to practice and compete. "If it causes any pain, though, stop."

Missy nodded.

After practice and during school, Missy finished her English descriptive paper and turned in all her homework. Smiling, she searched Google for hidden trails not shown on the map while also concerned about the time needed to uncover the secret treasure.

Echo, who sat by Missy in class, nudged her. "You finished with all assignments?"

"Yes, and I need fresh air. Got a half hour. I'm stepping outside."

"I'll join you."

Missy couldn't think of a better time to ask Echo about her brother. Halfway around the gym, she touched Echo's arm. "I have a question, and you don't have to answer if it's uncomfortable."

"Shoot."

"Do you have a brother named Sky?"

Echo's face went blank, and she nodded. "You saw the cross, I presume."

"I did. Can I ask what happened?"

"Like Coach Bell, he was also looking for Starr's grave. Despite having no knowledge of Sky's whereabouts, we made a cross by the cave where his knife was discovered."

A chill raced up Missy's back. Still, her brother was gone and she felt sorry about that. She hugged Echo. "I'm so sorry. I don't know what to say."

"Nothing to say. Sky may have fled without our knowledge. He lived carefree, indifferent to life, and left school during his senior year. He was never home. But when a friend saw the knife, he figured it was where he died or where he stopped to make his mark. Our friends and family hiked within a twenty-mile radius to see if we could find any signs of Sky's whereabouts. Nothing came up. He's on the national missing person list, you know."

Missy rubbed her hands. "Thank you for telling me. I've been warned numerous times about being alone here for too long."

"Smart choice." They went back to the gym.

Coach Pat and Coach Kirk lined the team up on the floor at the day's closing. "We rarely do this because you had the school break. Since there is a competition tomorrow, I want you to spend at least fifteen minutes strengthening your muscles slowly." Coach Kirk displayed a slow way of doing leg stretches. "Have at it and see you tomorrow at eight. The match is at ten."

Missy remembered she had left her bag in the classroom. She excused herself to run upstairs to get it. Reed entered from outside when she returned. He stopped her before she could take another step.

"Hi."

"Hi."

Reed hesitated, unsure of what to say. "Good luck tomorrow. Like in show business, break a leg." He offered a high-five.

"Thanks?" She scrunched her forehead and returned the gesture.

Reed nodded and went into the gym.

A hand slap? She waited a few seconds before she returned. After the team finished stretching, the coaches reiterated rest, to not over-stress their bodies, and go to bed early.

Maura switched to her complaining mood on the drive home in the car. "I feel like Cinderella being forced to work. I can do what I want." She changed the subject and blabbed about her and Brett's interests and how much they had in common.

Missy figured out Maura's personality was a bouncing ball. One minute, up and happy; next, grumpy. The ball was mostly on the ground, feeling sad and upset. She pretended to listen with an "ah" or "interesting" when needed.

Instead, she thought about Echo's story. It nagged her. Maybe it was Sky who'd dropped the arrow and had superpowers to leave the mirror and river messages. Maybe he was the one who'd carried her back to the tree when she'd been asleep.

Yes, her head had healed from the beating her fingers had given it a few days ago in the shower. She relaxed on the bed and doodled in her notebook.

Maura knocked on the bedroom door and entered.

"Hey, Miss. You looked a little troubled after practice today. What gives?" She sat by her once best friend.

"Confused." *Like you wouldn't know. You caused it, dummy.*

"Why?"

Should she tell her? Maura had a talent for turning any situation into a negative one. She made you feel worthless and put herself on top of the world. And if Missy didn't answer her, she'd get mad. "Lots of things." Her biggest fear was Maura finding out about her snooping around. She'd add more untruths.

"What type of things?" Maura twisted her hair.

Missy knew she'd keep asking until she answered. She sat and leaned back against the headboard. "Reed." She turned to a blank page and doodled more. "And Brandon."

"Whoa, there. Isn't it a no-go between you and Brandon?"

She looked at Maura with a painful expression. "Major trouble. We didn't want to admit deep feelings, and we're scared to let it show." She drew a heart and put a zigzag through it. "I'm done with men—all of them. Relationships suck sour lollipops."

"What's going on with Reed? And yesterday?" She took the pen from Missy's fingers and doodled by Missy's heart. "I see him take time to watch you when he comes to the gym, and he sits by you and Echo on Monday nights."

Julie, Missy could trust, but Maura? She was never sure. "I'm not attracted to Reed. I did not secretly meet with him yesterday."

"What happened?"

"It's stupid." *I'll try to keep her mind off yesterday.* "Today, Reed gave me a high-five and told me good luck tomorrow and to break a leg."

A smirk crossed Maura's face. "I bet he wanted to kiss your lips. I know he wants them." She drew lips on the paper and added a tongue hanging out.

"You're kidding me. Reed's not the only one sitting by us, and he hardly says boo when he sits by me. Echo's a motormouth and won't stop talking."

Maura patted Missy's leg. "You'll make the right decision. Dinner's ready." She left.

Her comment wasn't what she expected. It sounded like niceness coming out of her mouth. *Maybe Maura can be a caring person.*

She huffed. Perhaps there was a pattern. At home, Maura was okay. At practice, she tried to look demanding. She was a perfectionist. But Maura wasn't in control like she wanted it to seem. Missy desired to confront her about the reason for her meanness, but she wasn't prepared for conflict just yet.

***

After dinner, Missy watched TV with the Derringer family. It was the holiday season, and the TV stations played Halloween shows. Right before 7:00 p.m., the front doorbell rang. She was the closest and answered.

With his hands in his front pockets, Reed smiled. "The person I wanted to see. Come on, it's a clear sky full of stars, and I want to show you a neat spot by the river."

Butterflies and insecurity battled in her stomach. "Okay." She peered around the wall. "I'm stepping out." Mrs. Derringer waved okay.

"Show me what? Where are we going?"

"A hidden park."

"Are you kidnapping me?" Missy's heart skipped a beat.

"Trying to bite my head off? It's a short walk." Reed sounded disturbed.

They walked in silence until they reached a narrow opening in the shrubbery, revealing a small park by the Snake River.

"I'm confused. What's your reason for wanting to walk with me? I hardly know you." She felt stupid for the sarcastic response. "Sorry," she added, though Missy wondered if the walk would reveal a clue to where Jim was. She was tired of feeling a connection with him.

"It's okay. I wanted to show you one of my favorite places." Reed flashed his light around the area. The spot had two picnic tables, a pavilion, and a beautiful river view.

Next to the park, a boat dock and side deck provided a view of the waterfall. The waterfall wasn't large, but the landing was all rocks. She understood why both coaches didn't want anyone to swim in unmarked areas in the river.

Reed led her to a bench on the deck, and they sat. "This is where I go to escape. My dad's time-travel dreams are just the beginning of the story." He stared at the falls. "Don't get me wrong, but my dad believes he's cursed if he does anything bad. He believes Starr is waiting to pay him back for his death, even though he wasn't the person who killed him. Maybe Starr thought my dad could stop it, even though he had an arrow in his lung." Reed looked at her.

She wasn't sure what to say and hoped he wasn't leading her to feel sorry or guilty if she didn't kiss him to make him feel better. But he only watched her face.

"Why are you telling me this?"

"I saw the look in your eyes telling me you have a connection."

If he could read eyes, she'd have to wear sunglasses. "I'm confused about your dad's story. It stirred a hurtful past."

"I know. Want to talk about it?"

"No. It needs to stay buried. Why were you on the tracks?" She stared at the waterfall and begged it to wash away all memories . . . well, the terrible ones anyway. She could also ask Reed why he talked to Jim on Tuesday. Was Jim lost and needing directions? Perhaps Reed informed him of the drug-making location. She could walk in the daytime looking for the cave with a fishing pole.

They sat in silence for several minutes until Reed spoke. "How long have you practiced gymnastics?" He'd completely ignored her question about the tracks.

"A few years. I took classes and joined the junior high team at school. My dad built me a beam six inches off the ground and bought a couple of mats." Missy chuckled.

"What's funny?"

"My first attempt to do a cartwheel on the beam was horrible. My feet landed more than a foot away."

"Bonus; they hit the ground."

"True."

Out of nowhere, the question that had been bothering her since she arrived slipped from her lips uncontrollably. "Why am I—heck, why are all of us—warned not to be outside alone?"

Reed, not making eye contact, mentioned the incidents of people getting hurt or disappearing. He ended his explanation and glimpsed at his cell. "Time to go. The first competition tomorrow will be chaotic."

They walked back to the Derringers' house not speaking. Missy's brain ran wild. *Reed hid information, and his actions confused her. He'd only glanced at her once the entire night, saying goodnight and thanking her for coming with him. Sure, she was glad he'd shared with her the hidden spot. But why had he, anyway?*

In her room, she unfolded the map and realized they had strayed in an unmarked area. That made things more complicated. There could be other secluded areas by the river she needed to discover. Missy marked an X on the map where she was. Now the search would be more limited. *Double crap.*

But her emotions were suddenly in for a change when she stepped to the bathroom sink to brush her teeth. Now, fear filled her mind. On the mirror in bright red were the words: *Stay away. Trouble is near.*

Had she done something wrong? No. She wasn't a bad person. But someone else was. Reed!

While the Derringers remained engrossed in the movie, Missy found another spare room and phoned Julie. She couldn't rely on a quick response on a PM.

"Please don't kill me for not telling you."

"Telling me what?" Julie asked.

"I have my first meet tomorrow. I didn't want you to know and watch me blunder. But now I need you to come. I can't say more."

"You're getting crazy again, like you're possessed. Want me to come with your family?"

"No. Come in your car, please."

Julie agreed, and their conversation ended.

Chapter 12

The morning of the competition, Missy messed with her hair in the bathroom at the gym to ensure it stayed tight in the bun. She had worked tirelessly for months to grow long hair, but it was difficult to maintain. If she continued as a gymnast, her next plan was to get a bob cut.

She gave up on her hair and headed back to the floor. It was time to warm up. She saw her parents and Tommy sitting on the benches by the observation window by the gym's door.

"Hi, there. I'm nervous, but thanks for coming and watching me." She smiled at her parents, and little brother.

Julie had entered and joined the family. "Go win the golden trophy." Julie saluted.

Her mom replied with a hug. "You'll forget we're here, and you'll be fine."

"I agree with your mom." Her dad smiled. Tommy, being a cool tween, preferred an elbow bump.

"Got to go get ready." She waved and joined her team doing warm-ups.

***

Missy knew her routine for her first competition, though it was robotic not natural. Her movements were stiff on her floor routine, but she got second. She stepped forward once on the vault landing and placed second. A missed grip on the bars caused her to miss a move, and she got third. She hated beam and put no emotion into her actions and got fourth.

Still, the Owyhee County team came in second place out of five teams. She blamed Maura for the team not getting first—she'd fallen on her dismount from the bars—though she knew she was also to blame. Things were just easier when she blamed Maura.

The Macks congratulated her and offered a ride home before they left. Her reply was no. She wanted to show Julie her favorite hiking places.

Julie followed Missy back to the Derringers' and parked. "Why bring this up now instead of waiting until we're home?"

"We're going for a short walk."

"Where?"

"A secluded park."

"Before we get into your weird life, I want to say your team seems supportive and nice, minus one with a name we will not say. I never understood how the human body could be so limber."

"Not everyone's limber." She bent forward and pretended it hurt. "Snap, crackle, pop. But yeah, it's amazing. I admire myself at times." The girls laughed.

"How did you find this hidden spot?"

"Last night. Reed came by and showed me."

"Was Reed the nice-looking young gentleman with the brown hair?"

"Bingo."

"He bears a slight resemblance to Brandon. I can see how girls would fall for him."

"I guess." They walked for a few minutes before Missy stopped at the small opening. "Here it is." She pushed shrubbery out of the way to enter. "Looks different in the daytime." She led Julie to the bench by the river.

"We're out of range of eavesdroppers and peeping toms. Spill the beans," Julie coaxed.

"Remember last week when I told you about Coach Pat and his dreams? Reed said little, but his dad was trying to protect his wife, Chaundra. She has a connection with Starr." She glanced at Julie, who opened her mouth wide. "But here's the weird part. I saw a warning painted on the mirror twice, once at the Bells' house and in my bathroom. After a second look, it was gone."

"No way. Was it written in blood? What did it say?"

"It varied. Go home, you're in danger."

"Why are we here?"

"I feel this isn't the place to worry. I saw it Thursday, too."

"The mirror messages?"

"While hiking, I spotted the third one on the river." A splash drew Missy's attention to the river on her left. She watched the ripples the fish made.

"Is it signaling another message on the river?" Julie stood to see.

"Sorry, doesn't happen that way. I haven't had a noise to draw my attention. I do wish I had my pole." She joined Julie by the edge of the river.

"Girlfriend, your mind's getting worse."

Missy squeezed her head on both sides. "I don't get it. Why me? I thought the nightmares were over."

Julie touched her arm. "I wish I knew how to help you."

Taking a step toward the edge, she remembered the man-made trail at the picnic area. "Come on. I want to show you another place to visit."

"Any more trips as your chauffeur, I will charge."

"I'll buy you a treat at Dairy King."

Julie laughed and followed Missy's directions for a five-minute drive to another area by the Snake River.

"Our team's first potluck took place here. I wandered off as usual and found a hidden spot." They got out of the car. "Follow me."

"Is this another adventure like driving the motorcycles up the hill until I fall?"

"I hope not. But you wouldn't have fallen if you hadn't over-revved your motor."

"Whatever. Okay, I'll follow, but I'm not happy."

They reached the river's edge and turned left. The trail was narrow and seldom used.

"I've been on it once. You're fine." They walked a few steps. "Oh, I forgot to say who else popped into my dream with Starr."

"Now you're telling me about your haunted ghostly dreams when we're in the forest by the river? Why didn't you tell me before we entered this jungle or after?"

"I forgot."

"Great. Speak up, to end it quickly," Julie advised.

"Jim."

"It's a never-ending story in your life. I'm confused."

"Welcome to my personal life's journey." Missy paused as they reached the bend on the path and held out her hand to stop Julie. "Look." She pointed. "It's a homemade camp area. Come on."

"Oh no, I don't. I won't do that again. Dragging me to the pit in the night was eerie, but to a private campsite?

No sirree. Your bigfoot or lions, tigers, or bears. Nope." She put her hands on her hips.

"Give me a break. We're not in OZ land; it's daytime. I got a good scream if needed, you have your cell."

Julie placed her hand on her front pocket as a reassurance her cell phone was still there. "Fine. Okay."

The tiny shack had room for a cot and standing space. You could see someone had slept inside with the trash and sleeping gear.

"I wonder who lives here." Julie kicked around some candy wrappers.

"It wouldn't be Jim or Dwight. This is a setup for one person. It could be a homeless person. Guess we should go in case we run into him or a gorilla."

"Stop it," Julie warned.

A branch snapped. Missy and Julie stared at each other in fear. Missy pointed to the pile of firewood nearby and dragged Julie behind it and squatted. The footsteps got closer. Was it the person living here and noticed they were there?

Her heart continued to pound. She wondered if Julie could hear it. Suddenly, all grew silent, except for the sound of someone walking by as if leaving. Missy shifted to catch a glimpse of the unfamiliar man's back, not resembling Reed, Jim, or Dwight.

"It's nobody I know. He didn't look homeless either."

"Persisting will result in your eventual capture. I don't care if the person's close by. I'm gone." Julie took the lead and walked back to the picnic area. They sat on the bench to take a breather.

"Can I ask you a question about what just happened?"

"Of course, you can." Missy nodded.

"Do Murphy and Nampa have any similarities? The tractor, underground tunnels, and Jim? Or the person living in the forest?"

"There must be. Why else would Jim be here? And the fact Coach Pat has similar dreams as I do."

"I truly wish I could help. But I'm lost."

Missy's confusion deepened as she considered the scenario of Sky being present and still searching for a hidden treasure. She experienced a sudden, excruciating headache making her head feel like bursting. Interesting, too, was their names were similar—Starr and Sky. Was Echo's family an offspring of Starr?

"Take me home, Julie. I don't want to drive. Please, let's leave now and you can take me home."

They got up and jogged back to Julie's car, who then took her to the Derringers', where she got her belongings from her car and transferred them into Julie's Jeep.

Missy informed Julie about Reed's conversation with Jim, spotting Reed on the tracks, and speculated about a possible new drug spot in the mountains.

Julie covered the dull days and crazy times at school and added, "Life is boring without you in the neighborhood and at Nampa High."

"You have a horse to keep you company."

"True. Should I drive you home, or would you like to come over?

"Home."

They arrived at Mack's driveway.

"Come in for a minute." After chatting with her parents, they went into Missy's room. "I have mixed feelings, Julie. Love being on the team but uncomfortable with my living arrangements. I enjoy having my space here at home, but I don't like our neighborhood and school."

Julie's face turned sad.

"You know what I mean. You're here as a family. To tell you the truth, it doesn't matter where I go. My dreams or evil spirits follow me."

Julie sprang from the bed. "I got it."

"Got what?"

"You're dying to know how Brandon's doing. Call him now."

"Why?"

"Stop beating around the bush. Do it."

"You're supposed to tell me who Brandon sits with."

"Why don't you call and ask? It wouldn't hurt."

Missy felt scared by her inability to find words, but she mustered the courage to speak.

Julie handed the phone to her.

She swallowed and dialed the Miller's number.

"Hello." The voice was Rita, Brandon's mom. "Hello?"

She hung up. She couldn't speak; her mouth felt glued shut.

Julie sighed. "You goof head. Why didn't you ask for him?"

"I freaked out. I wouldn't know what to say. It's like I don't even know who Brandon is anymore."

"You could've bragged about your winnings today."

"No."

Julie slapped Missy's leg. "If they check their caller ID, they'll know who called."

"Duh. Stupid me. And I called the home number and not his cell. I mentally erased his number from my memory."

Julie left not long after, and Missy finished her laundry. She rested her hands on the washer, feeling the vibration as it spun. Doubt settled in her mind. *Quit, stay home. Stay out of Murphy. It's a waste of time.* Or was it a telepathic message from Chief Tso'ape-ha?

Chapter 13

"Glad we bought sleeping gear for both places. Driving back to Nampa to sleep during production would be a hassle." Dwight adjusted the double-sized air mattress on top of a cot to protect it from the ground.

"Agreed. It's living comfortably in the *down under* or above." Jim snickered as he stretched out on his bed. "I love being a nobody. I'm free." He inhaled from the pipe, and his brain tingled.

"And work in our own leisure time. Sleep whenever. It's like getting paid to be lazy," Dwight added.

"I wouldn't take advantage of it yet. We're still fresh back in Idaho and my grandparents gave the recipe of Twist to Rock's Edge. We'll work with Rock until we create our own improved version of Twist and venture out independently. We'll be the mother lode of money and make-you-feel-good' drugs."

"I saw a couple of small indents in the main cave. Might be items Rock's group left behind on accident." Dwight stood and tied his hiking boots.

"Go ahead. I'm enjoying my relaxation time." Jim stuffed his pipe with more Twist, lit it, and slept.

Buried Secrets

Twenty minutes passed until Dwight's yell echoed throughout the cave. "Jim! Jim! Get over here, quick! You'll never guess what I found!"

Jim's heart skipped a couple of beats. He gasped for air, sprinting to his friend's spot. Dwight was kneeling on the ground covered in dirt. "What do you want? I'm going to strangle you one day. Never wake me out of a deep sleep unless you find gold." He looked closer and saw indents where Dwight burrowed. Soft dirt, not hard like the rest of the cave.

"What do you think? The mother lode?" Dwight pointed.

Jim found a lever and dug in the hole as Dwight tried to scoop the dirt up with his hands furiously to stay caught up.

"Darn it, Dwight. Dig where I'm digging. Your dirt is landing where I've dug."

"Excu-u-use me." He switched positions and helped Jim make a separate pile of dirt on the side of the hole.

"I feel something!" Jim tapped the lever on some metal.

They brushed off more dirt and saw the top of the box. "We found it, we found it! Gold. Gold!"

"Let's get it out." Dwight rubbed his hands together.

Jim stood. "I'll get the shovel."

Carlos' shouting interrupted his action. "Hello, my cavemen. Come out, come out, wherever you are!"

Jim helped Dwight cover the box fast.

"What are you two doing digging into the cave's floor?" Carlos stood beside them.

"Oh, um, we thought we found an item, but we were mistaken." Jim pushed as much dirt as he could to cover the box.

"Children. You're acting like children. We'll fine-tune the machines and make you a winner," Carlos announced.

Dwight glanced at Jim and shrugged.

"You are going to do a profitable delivery tonight."

"Sounds great." Jim perked up.

"In Portland," Carlos finished.

"Portland? Tonight? A long drive tonight?" Jim surreptitiously glanced back longingly to where the box lay.

"Take catnaps at the rest areas when needed."

"But the Blue Mountains are windy and dark. We might hit a deer."

"Deal with it." Carlos took a palm-sized piece of metal out of the box he held. "This will speed up the dehydration time." He attached it to the motor. "And after Portland, you're headed off to Seattle. Get to work." And he left.

Jim waited for Dwight at the cave's entrance and enjoyed the cool breeze and the sound of the river. They sorted, dried, crushed, and bagged a ten-pound box of fresh Twist in Five hours. He was frustrated they had to leave now for delivery when their treasure was in the cave.

Leaving in the early evening and despite their ongoing argument about the trip, they switched places at the halfway mark to stay awake.

Dwight wished they had brought along the box of gold for safekeeping, but Jim thought it would have fallen into the wrong hands if they had. Dwight was concerned that Carlos might find the discovery before their return.

Chapter 14

After putting the last dish in the dishwasher, Mrs. Mack noticed Missy tying her shoes. "Ready to go?"

"Ready as I can be." She looked at her duffle bag. "Dang, I forgot my homework. I'll be out in a minute." Her mom dried her hands and left to start the car.

Returning with her homework in hand, Missy clicked her seatbelt and changed the radio station from oldies to the Top 40s. "Remember to park in the gym area. It's a closer walk to the high school office."

"Yes, Your Highness." Mrs. Mack tapped her fingers on the steering wheel to the beat of the music.

"Mom, you're the best. Glad you like my music, too." When they arrived at the school, Missy waited for her mom to find a spot to park. "I'll be back in less than five minutes." She hurried to the school's office and turned in her assignments.

On her way back to the car, she saw Brandon by his truck. If she turned to go back inside, he'd see her. Plus, she knew he'd seen her mom's car. She pulled her shoulders back and continued.

Brandon closed his truck door and placed the strap of his duffle bag on his shoulder. He smiled. "Hey, you back in Nampa?"

She stopped a few feet in front of him. "Nope. I'm still in Murphy. I turned in my homework."

Brandon looked her over with his gorgeous eyes. "Do your coaches keep you busy? Do you get along with your teammates?" Brandon raised his eyebrows.

"I've made a couple of friends. It helps me keep positive motivation. And it's a break from being Maura's shadow. I watch TV with the family, and I like her parents." *Hopefully, he doesn't think I'm rambling like a chatterbox.*

He looked at his watch. "Got to get back to class. Take care, and maybe we can get together in your free time." Brandon turned, presumably heading to the weight room.

"Sure. See you." Missy slid into the car.

"Were you talking to Brandon?"

"Yep."

Mom was silent.

"Perhaps chocolate would be nice," Missy concluded. "I'm not in a hurry."

They stopped at a convenience store and bought Almond Roca to devour on their short trip. The taste of it, all smooth and chocolaty, always changed her mood.

Missy walked onto the floor mat during warm-up five minutes late and sat by Echo. Coach Pat gave her a stern look. She'd readied herself to get scolded but lucked out.

Echo leaned over. "I was ready for the coach to yell at you. He makes me break out in a sweat."

"I was prepared and would have taken it like a grown-up." She saw Maura do the typical eye roll. Reed folded his arms. His expression was one of, 'You're asking for it.'

So, what? Being a gymnast was more difficult than she'd expected. Given the chance, she would escape from it. Her body felt the pain, and her mind felt the stress.

The short practice was dull as Missy didn't put effort into it. For her mental stability, she asked Echo and Vallie for a ride home. Once settled in the car, she leaned forward from the back seat. "Do you know what your brother was searching for?"

"Sky kept to himself. Our personalities clashed more often than not. Vallie might know more. They got along. The search for Starr's grave may have been a cover for a bank robbery."

"More because I was the youngest baby sister and easy to pick on," Vallie explained. "We played make-believe, imagining a spaceship journey to a different world in search of treasures. He promised to search the world and return for me once he found the perfect spot. On a Sunday morning, he hugged me, announced his adventure, and never came back." Vallie wiped her nose with her jacket.

Echo pulled into the Derringers' driveway. "We figured he took off to another state, changed his name, and started a new life."

"Thank you for the ride and the information. Again, I'm sorry for the emotional stuff."

Echo shrugged. "No problem. Life goes on. I've learned to look on the positive side, so I'm not depressed."

Missy waved and walked inside right when Maura drove in and parked. As Missy feared, Maura's attitude was terrible. Her mom had gone with Jake for a dentist appointment, so the attitude shield was gone.

Maura stormed into the kitchen and stood in front of Missy. Maura's sister, Sandy, was already there.

"How do you do it?" Maura asked. "Five minutes late, and you don't even get an eyebrow raise?"

Maura retrieved a mug from the cupboard and mixed chocolate into her milk. "I was one minute late last week coming out of the bathroom before warm-up, and I had to run two extra laps." She tossed the spoon she'd used into the sink. "What have you done to butter up the coaches?"

"I don't know what you mean. They know I drive here from Nampa. There's slow traffic, you can get behind, lots of reasons." Missy picked up a napkin to fiddle.

"Let me see. Did you drive on Bigfoot Avenue to the gym to see if the big hairy guy was mowing his lawn?"

Sandy walked over to Maura and slapped her butt. "Shut up. Why do you pick on Missy? She hasn't done anything to you." She gave Maura a 'you're an idiot' look and left to watch TV in the family room.

For a moment, Maura looked dumbfounded, gasped, and ran outside to the barn. A few minutes later, Missy saw Maura galloping around in the field on her horse.

Sandy returned to the kitchen. "I'm clueless about what's happening with Maura. She's always been on the nagging side, but it's been miserable lately." She retrieved a cookie from the jar. "The move, missing Ally, PMSing? Sorry. Want one?"

"No, thanks. It's okay. I've learned to deal with Queen Attitude Maura." To get ready for dinner at the Bells', she headed to her room.

Yep, Sandy was right about Maura acting worse. Maybe she had a mental problem. Perhaps not having her Ally next door was killing her. Missy assumed Chaundra would appreciate her assistance with dinner setup, so she went over to her place.

Once there, she rang the doorbell, hoping they didn't mind her early arrival. Chaundra opened the door. "What a surprise. Come on in." She wiped her hands on the apron wrapped around her waist and smiled.

"You need help with dinner?" She followed Chaundra to the kitchen.

"Lucky for you, I'm set, or I'd love the help. I had prior commitments over the weekend and couldn't find time to prepare. Tonight is the simple build-your-own sandwiches, soup, fruit, veggies, chips, and the must-have shrimp. Sound good?" She pointed at the fridge. "And confession time. I had brownie dough in the freezer for last-minute treats. Can't miss having dessert."

"You are an angel." Missy saw the pots on the stove and the makings needed for sandwiches. "Looks yummy, and I'm not picky. A bowl of cereal satisfies me for dinner, and a piece of cold pizza for breakfast."

"Next time." She stirred the pot of soup.

Missy nodded. "You don't mind me asking a question, do you?"

"About the soup?"

"No. Another one."

"Ok. Shoot."

"Pat's search is connected to Starr. What is it?"

Chaundra shrugged. "Starting the story will take all night. Besides, you know you'll worry about it." She pointed at a chair by the big window. "Go make yourself at home. The chair by the fireplace is comfy, and Reed will join us soon."

"Thanks." Missy sat, observed the river waves, and hoped she hadn't upset Chaundra. She heard footsteps coming up the stairs a few seconds later. Reed.

"Hey, want to see my pet?" He grabbed her hand and pulled her out of the chair.

"I guess I have no choice." She slipped her hand free as they reached the stairs.

"Nope." He waited for her at the bottom of the stairs. "I wanted to see the tracks tonight. Starr might show he exists." He continued past a big TV in a gathering room. "Come this way."

"Sure, fine." *Maybe he'll show me where he goes during the night.*

"Great. But beware of my bedroom. I try to keep it clean."

She laughed.

"Why laugh? What's funny?"

"Dude, you haven't seen any room as messy as mine. I'm uncertain if the shirt I have on is clean or requires an urgent wash."

Reed sniffed the air by her. "Your shirt's clean."

"Ugh. Gross." They laughed.

His room appeared tidy. In the corner, a small pile of clothes coexisted with a neatly made bed and a stack of papers on the desk. On the wall, shelves displayed trophies, ribbons, and photos of Reed and his team.

"Way to go on your awards. It must feel good." She looked at him.

"It did then, but now it doesn't matter. There's more to life besides trophies."

"Really?"

"Who needs the stress? And anyway, life's too short." He walked over to the head of his bed.

She wisely kept silent. It wasn't her business.

He pointed to the antlers on the wall above his bed. "See the long, round, scabby-looking skin?"

She went closer to look. "Dead animal?"

"Snakeskin."

"Snakeskin?"

"Yep."

"You're telling me you have a snake?"

"Yep."

"A garter snake?" She scanned her surroundings, hoping to spot a small snake she could hold in her palm. She was fine with bugs and regular animals, but having a snake slithering freely in a bedroom was definitely not preferable.

"Sorry, garter snakes don't get as big as boa constrictors." Reed looked under his bed. "She might be hiding in my closet. This morning, she ate a rat, so she'll be lying low for a while."

"Did you catch her, or is she a pet-store snake?" A wave of fear washed over Missy, yet she remained composed. She could picture the snake easing up her legs and around her neck to strangle her. She shivered. "Does it have a name?"

"Boa."

"Cute." She glanced around nervously. "I believe it's time to go." Finding her way quickly back to the chair by the fireplace, she bit at her finger. Her biggest fear was the team spotting her exiting the basement alongside Reed.

She looked out the window. Maura had tied her horse to the side of the barn in the Bells' back yard, and Brett stood beside her in deep conversation. Maura flapped her arms like a chicken trying to fly.

"As Maura's Life Turns, the soap opera." Missy giggled.

"What's funny?" Echo sat on the fireplace's hearth.

"Look." She pointed. "Maura and Brett are having a serious conversation. It's Brett's turn to run on the hamster's wheel." He paced back and forth in front of Maura and her horse.

"I'm curious about what they're arguing about."

"With Maura, it's always something stupid. Perhaps it's just a strand of her hair out of place." Her attention was drawn to Maura and Brett, who were sharing a quick hug and kiss outside the window. "I bet she told Brett it was her way or the highway." They held hands and walked toward the house. Missy swore Maura knew she was watching her. She smiled like she had won first prize in a competition.

***

During dinner, Pat and Kirk gathered everyone's attention. "Great news we want to share." Kirk smiled.

"Making headlines, we earned tickets to travel and compete globally," Vallie said as she raised her arm in victory.

"No, but it would be nice if it happened." He held up his hand. "Murphy will have a Halloween dinner dance Saturday night on the thirtieth. Also, there is a competition happening on the same day. It's a perfect place to stay in town for the activities. It draws a sizeable crowd from the surrounding towns with dancing, hayrides, a haunted house, and a corn maze."

"Sounds fun. But I'm not sure I want to enter the haunted house." Echo shivered. "I went to one with my brother in sixth grade and got scared out of my wits. I swear it wasn't an actor who chased me with an ax."

Missy recalled seeing actual ghosts and didn't want to re-encounter them. "I understand. But dancing and the corn maze sound fun."

Echo nodded. "Will any of the team guys ask us to the dance?" She gawked at Rich from Team Four.

"Don't know." Missy looked at Rich. "Ask him now."

Echo blushed. "It shows I like him. Too easy. I can't help it. You saw how he helped me on the beam when we combined groups the other day."

"Go ask," Missy coaxed.

Echo laughed. "I will."

Rich smiled as she approached.

Echo returned and retrieved her plate. "He said he'd love to."

"I knew it."

Echo returned to sit by Rich.

Reed sashayed over and sat by Missy. "What do you say?"

"Depends on what you ask." *I bet he's curious about my past with Starr.*

"Hit the dinner and dance with me?"

"It's a deal, as long as we avoid the haunted house."

Reed leaned back. "What? No scary boos in the house?"

"No."

"Hayride and corn maze off your schedule?"

"Hayride can take a hike, but I can do the corn maze unless you turn into Dracula and suck my blood. Bahahaha." She raised her upper lip and sucked in the air.

"Oh, it might happen. My true self might come out."

"It better not because my legs are strong enough to kick you." She gave him a 'beware' look.

Reed placed both hands on his heart. "You broke my heart. I'm bleeding to death."

"Yeah, right," Missy mocked.

"The haunted house is a bunch of silly stuff, anyway. I have other plans you might like better instead of the maze. Don't worry. Nothing dangerous will happen. And I'll keep my teeth to myself." He left for the buffet table.

Missy checked on Echo. They were in deep conversation. The fire sparked, and a strong smell of maple wood filled the air. It reminded her of camping trips. The Macks hadn't camped the previous summer, which was sad. In the Cascade Mountains north of Boise, they owned a cabin spot in the Silver Creek Plunge camping area with a storage unit for their motorcycles and snowmobiles.

Silver Creek was a natural heated pool. Steam rose from the water, even in the summer. The snack bar by the pool was what she liked best. Chick-o-Stick candy was the best, along with her other favorites of Snickers, Kit Kat, and Peanut M&Ms. She knew she was a chocoholic.

Reed put a plate of small desserts in front of her as Missy watched the fire and was dreaming. "What's this?" She pointed at the goodies.

"It's an official celebration for our first date." He split a brownie in half and offered a piece to her. She snatched it and popped it into her mouth.

"Thanks. You sure there's not snakeskin in the filling?"

"Now I can say gross." Reed squinched his nose.

"I could get fat with your mom's cooking." She chewed the moist brownie.

Maura walked over to Missy and interrupted her and Reed's conversation. "I'll walk home with you since I don't want to ride my horse in the dark."

"Go ahead on your own. I got plans." *Oh, I love driving Maura's brain crazy. It's payback time.*

She gave the cold eye to both and left.

"I'm ready to go see your secret place."

Reed stood, and Missy followed him to the deck and down the stairs. They passed Maura as she untied her horse, waved, and continued to walk to the path by the Snake River.

"The safe spot to stand by the tracks is behind the Derringers'. One reason tonight is good is it's a full moon, and you're close to home."

"I know where it is. Can you explain the connection between the train and Starr?

"He was killed and buried around here. Remember what my dad said? His spirit still likes to run with his horse alongside the train when it passes by." He led Missy to a flat spot across the bridge. He pointed to the right. "If he comes, he'll ride around the point of Cooper's Bend on his horse. Amtrak should come any minute."

They stood there for a few minutes with no Starr or train. "Must be running behind schedule. Amtrak's hardly ever late."

Another minute passed, and the horn's distant sound echoed. She got excited.

The train came and went. "Maybe Ol' Chief Starr knew we were watching and was too scared to come out and play." Reed put his arm over Missy's shoulder. She shivered. "Cold?" He drew her closer.

She was even more lost and confused. "No, a muscle spasm."

On their way to the Derringers' front door, Reed stopped by the side of the house, pulled her closer, and wrapped both arms around her waist. "I hoped you were cold so I could keep you warm."

She kept her arms at her sides, unsure whether to return his hug or stand still. Reed eased back and cupped her face with his hands.

"I'm fine."

"I know you are." He leaned forward and kissed her.

She pushed back. "Slow down."

"Why?"

"I'm not ready to jump into a relationship. I'm still a kid."

"You look pretty grown up to me," Reed observed.

The words lingered in the air, heavy and lifeless.

"What do you want from me? Are you trying to trick me into going out alone at night? Does this explain your interest in going to the corn maze with me in a couple of weeks?"

She turned to leave, but Reed grabbed her hand.

"No. I like you and thought you'd want to learn about Starr. Please trust me. I'm not using you. There are numerous connections to Starr that I cannot fully describe. Confusing, but he'll lead us to an answer my mom needs."

Missy bit her lower lip. "I'm not confused and not at all surprised there's more." She scanned her surroundings for a dead branch to grasp. "I'm going to tell you about an experience I had a year ago. Not certain if it will aid or indicate my understanding." She found a twig.

"Tell me." Reed nudged her on the side.

"I got lost in a dark tunnel and . . ." A chill ran through her body, and suddenly, she couldn't speak. "I-I-I've got to go. Good night."

She headed toward the front of the house.

"Wait!"

But it was too late. She'd already gone inside and slammed the door. She was safe. And Reed? He was outside, more than likely wondering what had just happened. It didn't bother her until she reached the bathroom and glanced at her reflection.

You disobeyed me. Stay away.

Chapter 15

"I can't believe it's Tuesday, and we have free time. It's been a long time since Saturday. When Carlos and Rock want business done, they want it done, like, yesterday." Dwight sat by the indent on the cave's wall in Murphy. "We get to see what's in the treasure chest."

"I suggested we maintain a favorable relationship with both parties by assuming a servile role temporarily. It will get better soon, I promise," Jim stated. "Last night, I remembered my grandparents had another recipe I haven't tried yet because the current one is doing fine. Soon, we will experiment and get a better quality of Twist to die for."

"I love the sound of it. Let's dig away."

In a few minutes, Jim and Dwight pulled the box out. Two metal locks kept the lid from opening.

"Now what?" Jim pulled on both in the hope they would unlatch. The locks were rusty and held firm.

"Back at my office, if it's still there, is a small corner dresser. Inside the drawer is a lock-breaking kit. Perfect for cars brought in with no keys."

"Let's go. I'm hungry, and a cheeseburger sounds perfect."

Jim's hands were on fire. He swore and dropped the box back in the hole as best he could. Looking at his hands he saw nothing. "Did you feel the heat?" He blew on his hands.

"No. And stop dropping things. You might have broken a priceless collectible."

Jim glared at Dwight and grunted. "The box is staying here. Our luck, it will explode in the car."

***

Jim's anxiety about sleeping in Nampa led him and Dwight to return to Murphy in the middle of the night. His gut tensed as they set up the lanterns in the cave with the lock kit.

Dwight hummed as he scooped out the loose dirt around the box.

"You're tooting a happy fairy tale song digging by a hot box. Don't you feel the heat?" Jim asked.

"Nope. But my hands aren't hugging it either. I'm barely touching it." He grabbed a rag from his tool container and placed the box on solid ground. He found the correct tool pin, moved it around in each lock, and clicked them. "You want to open it, or should I?"

"Me, of course. I'm in charge." Jim rubbed his hands on his thighs. "Here goes." He squatted, leaned forward, and removed both locks. He lifted the lid. Sparks shot out like fireworks and the lid dropped and closed.

"What the heck was that?" Dwight shrieked.

"Shut up. Let me open it all the way." Jim popped his knuckles and pushed the lid open. "See? Nothing to worry about." He took a drink of soda.

"A ghost." Dwight whispered.

Jim glanced back at the box, watching as black smoke seeped out and shaped itself into a face. The mouth opened and hands with long fingers reached out and forcefully shoved him onto his back, briefly rendering him unconscious. When Jim opened his eyes, his head felt like loose gravel and he raised his arms to stop the commotion.

"Are you breathing? Are you dead?" Dwight leaned over him, his fingers about to touch his eyelids.

"Keep your hands off my face!" He fenced Dwight's hands away.

"What happened? I thought you were dead!"

"If I wasn't breathing, I wouldn't tell you, nitwit." He sat and looked at the box, unsure of what had occurred.

"The ghost might be protecting gold." Dwight eyed the box and then returned his gaze to Jim.

"I don't care what's in there. You check if you want to know. If not, close, lock, and bury the blasted thing." Jim crawled up onto his knees, his eyes never leaving the box.

"I ain't going anywhere near it." Dwight shook his head. "No sir. I'm not touching it."

"You piece of chicken crap. I'm wounded, and you don't care."

"I do care, but I'm not touching it." He inched himself closer to the exit.

"Fine. I hope you're cursed for being mean." Jim crawled over to the box. He touched the locks to ensure they weren't hot and picked them up. He used his foot to close the lid, locked the box, and walked backward toward Dwight as if he needed to monitor the cover to make sure it didn't open again.

"Time to go! I don't care if we never return," Jim took a few steps toward the exit.

"Shouldn't we bury the box?"

"You can kick it back into the hole."

"I guess it's safe." Dwight used his foot to push the dirt partially on top of the box. "Done. Let's go."

Jim left before Dwight finished, but the lingering thoughts of what happened plagued Dwight late into the night.

Chapter 16

Missy didn't see Reed at Tuesday's practice. He either didn't want to see her or had other obligations like finding Starr's grave on his own or selling drugs. She was confused about Reed or how she liked him. Was she using him to find Starr's hidden treasure as an excuse to see if he was on drugs or dealing them? Did she genuinely like him, or was he a substitute for Brandon?

She pushed hard to finish her homework early during study time and would do more snooping around at the Derringers'.

Her strength on bars and vault showed in her practice. Her thighs had firmed as she continued to do the weights. Hiking had helped too. Exercise and mystery-solving only occurred once a week, posing a challenge to fit them in.

Coach Pat snapped his fingers. It was the end of practice. "All right, team. You've improved, which was evident in last week's competition." He looked at Coach Kirk. "Because of a cold front coming in on Saturday, we are switching our day outing for tomorrow."

"Day outing? Like to the zoo or park?" Echo whispered in Missy's ear. "It sounds like a grade-school fieldtrip."

Missy shrugged.

"We will meet here at the gym early in the morning at six. Dress in warm layered clothes and toss in a hat," Coach Pat said.

Everyone looked at each other, confused.

Coach Kirk laughed. "Oh, a smart choice is wearing warm socks and hiking boots. If you don't have boots, tennis shoes are a must." Turning around, he headed toward the foyer door. "Don't be late." He stared at them for a moment. "And don't forget a swimsuit and a towel. See you tomorrow."

"Bring a swimsuit?" Missy looked at Maura, who laughed like she didn't care.

"This doesn't sound good to me. What's our destination and plans?"

Echo made a fist. "He puts us through too much. I quit if it's shoveling poop out of his horse stables."

Missy got her belongings out of her cubby and waited for Maura.

"Good news is he never said anything about bringing food or water," Echo continued. "The day won't be difficult or lengthy." She retrieved her items. "I'll see you bright and early."

Maura walked by the lockers. "Ready, Missy?" Brett was with her.

Missy followed like a sad, lost puppy. It didn't matter who Maura was with. Maura hardly acknowledged her presence unless there was nothing else for her to do—she was the third wheel and almost invisible.

Maura slammed her car door. "I hate surprises. And this one by Coach Kirk takes the cake. Do you have any clues?"

"I have no idea and don't want to waste my time guessing." Missy bet Reed had planned the day's activities, and she was relieved that was likely the reason he hadn't been at the gym, not that he was avoiding her. Before Maura had a chance for a comeback, Missy continued. "Maybe it'll be an obstacle course and race. I can see it happen with hay bales to jump over and ropes to swing on. Sounds fun."

"It's too girlish for me." Maura snorted.

"Oh, crap."

"What gives?" Maura started the car and pushed play on the CD player.

"I don't want to drive to my house tonight to get a swimsuit."

"Hey, Sandy is taller than you but around the same size. I'm sure she'll let you borrow one," Maura said.

"I hope so." It surprised her that Maura wanted to help.

Sandy let Missy try on two swimsuits at home. The dark red one-piece suit with no high bottom cut satisfied her.

A broken night's sleep put Missy on edge the following day. Her dreams were about her team competing in the cornfield. They held the balance beam routine over the Snake River. The catfish with Dracula's teeth bit your legs off if you fell.

When the alarm rang, the worst nightmare hit. Four hours of sleep would keep her intact until midafternoon, and then she'd turn into a grumpy zombie.

Mrs. Derringer prepared breakfast sandwiches the night before and stored them in the fridge to heat up before leaving. Maura, as usual, drove. Missy bet she'd want her to find a ride home so she could go off with Brett into the wild frontier. They arrived last among the team.

Missy went over to stand by Vallie, Echo, and Rich. "My body doesn't like to sleep before an unplanned day."

"No problem for me," Vallie said.

Kirk broke the silence. "Gather around, people."

They stood in a circle with both coaches in the middle. "Workouts and doing the same daily routines get boring. Am I right?"

The team cheered.

"So, we've added a little fun with an adventurous workout. Everyone, bring your swimsuit and a towel!"

More 'yeses' shouted out.

"As soon as our transportation arrives," Coach Kirk directed his arm to the parking lot, "we'll be going."

"Has anyone else heard of Jump Creek Canyon?" Pat asked.

Missy had but hadn't visited it.

"You're about to see an amazing and unique rock formation with a splendid waterfall. Two hiking trails are available: one leading to the mountain top and the other along the creek to the pond on the bottom. No, we aren't swimming. If it were summer, we would."

"Good," Maura snapped.

Kirk continued, "We are climbing both." He finished his speech and let the team mingle until their rides came.

Echo's shoulder bumped Missy. "Have you seen Reed?"

She rubbed her hands together. "Not since Monday night." Three Suburbans pulled into the parking lot and interrupted the conversation. Coach Doug, Coach Aaron, and Reed parked their vehicles.

Pat spoke out. "Pick a car. It will take close to an hour to get to our destination." He showed the team a small box. "Snack on a protein bar as you go."

Buried Secrets

Echo, Rich, Gwynn, Leslie, and Missy headed toward Reed's vehicle.

"I'll get a little lonely riding up front by myself." Reed lifted his eyebrows. "There's an open seat."

Missy hesitated a second, then retraced her steps and got in front. She wasn't sitting close to Reed like Echo and Rich were in the back seat, but she was by him.

"You played hooky yesterday. Sick?" She raised her eyebrows.

"Nope, getting ready for today and working on the Halloween party." Reed cranked up the radio volume.

On route, they passed Givens Hot Springs. She bet they were going there after their hike.

As they reached the outside of the canyon, the paved road turned into dirt. They traveled down a small embankment to park in a lower spot. "You can leave your bags in the car." Reed approached Missy after she exited and closed the door. "You're going to love this." He touched her cheek.

Pat got the team's attention. "The trail's first segment spans roughly a quarter mile. There we'll see the waterfalls and the pond. We will cross over the creek, so be careful. It's slippery on the rocks." He led the way. "The cliffs are formed from volcanic rock. There are big volcanic gas pockets to climb into and sleep in if needed."

"They're the perfect size for birds and small critters," Kirk butted in. "But there are bigger ones for people. And, of course, there's a porta-potty if needed."

He pointed to a rest area with two picnic tables. Currently, there were no takers.

Missy stayed in the back of the group to view the scenery. Reed noticed and joined her. "Looking?"

She watched a prairie falcon land on a tree. "For anything I can see."

"Don't you want to stay with the team?"

"Nope. I'm a nature fanatic and love taking in all I can. Even in the semi-mountain desert, there is beauty."

"Just like you."

"What?"

"Nature is as beautiful as you." Reed pulled her close and kissed her.

"Stop. We'll get in trouble."

"Nah, they can't see us." He kissed her again.

A few minutes later, they made it to the waterfalls. What a sight. The falls' mist chilled the air.

"Can we explore the side trails and caves on our way back?" Rick asked.

"Yes," Pat answered.

Some of the team explored the small caves, while others crossed the river to examine the mountain openings. Missy noticed the two coaches, Doug and Aaron, stayed back by the cars to set up lunch.

"Lucky the rattlesnakes aren't out. It's too cold for them." Echo sighed with relief. "I encountered one out here a few years ago. Blessed be my brother who saved me. Still have the rattle as a reminder to keep my eyes open."

"Thank you for the information," Missy said.

Pat announced it was time to return to the base.

"My stomach growled." Missy covered her gut as if to mute the sound.

"I heard it." Echo covered her ears.

Pat whistled to get the team on the move.

Maura hurried from the back and paused at Missy's side. "Did you see your Chief Ghost Friend in the haunted caves?" She smirked and continued to the front.

"She aimed it right at your heart." Echo's voice sounded hurt.

"I'm used to it. I'm not in the mood to start an immature spat." She stopped speaking and looked over at Echo. Echo had done nothing wrong by saying what she did. She would just let Maura's comment go.

"Now I know why Doug and Aaron stayed back," she said, pointing to the extra tables with folding chairs by the picnic tables stacked with food.

"I was hoping we were going to eat." Echo rubbed her stomach.

The smell of food lingered in the air. "This's what you did yesterday?" She looked at Reed.

He smiled and led her to the table to dig in. They talked about their discoveries and ate pancakes, eggs, sausage, bagels, orange juice, and hot chocolate.

A half-hour later, the team helped clean up the trash, folded the tables and chairs, and loaded them back into the vehicles.

Kirk stood on top of a picnic table. "The next hike is trickier. Steep and narrow. Take your time and watch where you put your feet. You don't want to step on a loose rock and slip." He led the way up the small hill to the upper parking lot, where the trail started.

Missy remained at the end of the line. She desired to savor the view at her own pace.

"Be careful. I don't want you to get hurt," Reed said. "But I won't mind catching you if you fall." He winked.

Her hands on her hips and half-jokingly, she replied, "Stop saying that and making me feel more of a klutz than I am, mister."

"Yes, ma'am. But seriously, be careful. The rocks are wet here, too."

The hike wasn't as bad as she'd heard. Right at the trail's peak, everyone halted, and Maura shouted back to

Missy. "Your friend gave us all a haunted visit." She laughed and continued around the curve.

"Haunted visit?"

The word *haunted* had gotten too communal for Missy to hear. "I have no idea what she means," she said to no one in particular. They stopped where Maura was and turned to the area she pointed at.

Reed followed her observation at the rocky mountainside off to the left. "To me, it looks like the mountain is watching us."

One side of the mountain bore the likeness of a Native chief's face. The eyes appeared disturbingly lifelike. "Holy crap. Is Starr buried there?" Missy asked.

"He might be, and why was Maura bothering you?"

"I'd rather not discuss it." She glanced one more time at the Native head before continuing her walk.

Reed kept silent for a few minutes. "Have you had dreams of Starr, like my dad?"

She hesitated. "No. I suppose it's time to say what I intended to tell you on Monday night. I've dealt with another Native American who has been an angel. It might be the previous local chief that Starr was under before he started his own path. Heck, it could be Starr himself acting like a different person. He was nice and gave me light in a tunnel to avoid a person I despise who chased me. But he said his name was Chief Tso'ape-ha. And every time I see a Native American picture, I see him."

"And I thought my dad's visions were off the wall."

She knew he wasn't being mean to her, but now, along with the team, she'd be seen as a lost cause because of Maura. She picked up a rock to hold or, more like, squeeze. Reed kept walking and Missy hoped he felt rotten.

The group reached the top of the waterfalls. "I can't believe people jump from here to the pond. It doesn't look deep enough." Echo peeked over the edge.

"You can try it now," Maura snarled.

Echo laughed back. "I'll go after you."

Missy dropped her rock over the edge and watched it bang on the mountainside before it hit the water. She had to stop herself from following behind. The face on the mountain and the comments from Maura and Reed destroyed her mood, prompting her desire to leave.

"How could a mean person be nice to me?"

"Nice to you? Who, Maura?" Reed had stayed close to her by the mountain's edge.

"Never mind. I've told you too much already." She paused to admire the mountainside, filled with volcanic indents and caves. *Was it possible an evil person could turn good, like Darth Vader? Maybe Starr did. But how did Jim Forst tie in? Was he related to Starr?* Her goal was to let the past stay buried, unlike her parents' past. Not a fun experience to go through.

They headed back to the bottom of the mountain to meet their group. It was a silent walk, but the sentiment was mutual. No hard feelings.

Maura found her way to Missy. "Wherever you go, the tractor ghost follows you. You're possessed." She went back to Brett and her gymnast followers.

"You have more buried secrets," Reed said.

"And in my wishes, they'll stay buried for good." Missy entered the Suburban and watched the desert pass to their next destination at Givens Hot Springs. She'd been there a few times. She couldn't stand the heat of the natural water after a half-hour of being in it. However, that's exactly what she would be doing soon.

Before they went into the building, Echo pulled her aside. "Are you having fun? What was Maura yelling at you about?"

"Loved the surroundings and the waterfall. Maura likes to share stuff I've been through."

"She's foul."

"If there was a larger percentage of one hundred, she'd have it times one thousand."

Missy looked over at Reed. He was carrying on a conversation with a couple of other assistant coaches. "She seems okay at home. It's when Maura's in a crowd that she's mean."

"You and Reed get in a fight?"

"No. I don't expect anything from Reed." Honestly, she was glad to have a break. Discussing the upcoming meet and the shift to hiking, she couldn't help but burst into laughter again.

The team got their swimsuit bags, changed, and entered the hot pool. Missy waited until the bathroom was empty to put on Sandy's suit. After dressing, she looked in the mirror. It fit okay, but it wasn't her. She didn't want to swim. She wanted to walk instead. Nobody would miss her. She dressed, shoved the swimsuit in Maura's bag, and went outside.

Missy didn't tell the coaches she was leaving. She didn't care. She needed to clear her mind. Being a fast walker, she figured three miles in an hour. It'd take her six hours to walk the eighteen miles to the Derringers', and she was sure they'd be finished swimming in two.

Seeing the face on the mountain left her with an unclear feeling. Was she required to confirm the presence of a nearby cave? It might be a warning or a natural anomaly.

Two and a half hours later, reality hit Missy. Leaving hadn't been right. She should've told the coaches and hoped Maura had opened her mouth.

Hearing a vehicle approaching from behind, she immediately recognized the sound. Reed pulled to the side of the road in front of her. The remaining two rigs from the team drove past and honked. Embarrassed, she opened the door and sat.

"What do you think you're doing? Crazy people drive on this road out in no-man's-land. Why didn't you tell us?"

Missy looked back at Echo, who gave a slight smile. She was uncertain about her actions and words. "I'm walking and didn't see any crazy people except my reflection. Sorry, I kept my mouth shut."

"You're lucky. Vallie saw you take off when she went outside. After a short walk, I thought you'd be back. I didn't want to leave the pool and chase after you."

"I'm fine." She watched the bland horizon out the window until their return to the gym. The rigs were parked, and like three running faucets, the teammates poured out the open doors.

Holding Brett's hand, Maura made an audience for herself and yelled across the parking lot. "Missy, can you find a ride home? Or you can finish your walk. You're closer now. Might take you another hour!" She patted the hood of her car and smiled at Brett.

"I'll give you a ride. I wouldn't want to be in the same car with her either," Echo added.

"Thank you." She followed Echo to her car but was interrupted by Coach Pat.

"Missy."

It was all she needed. Head down, she went over to Coach Pat and Coach Kirk.

"Not a smart choice, was it? What were you thinking when you left? You are under our care. Your parents signed a release. We're responsible for you! What would your parents say if something had happened to you?" Coach Pat's tone was firm and serious.

Coach Kirk's voice was softer. "We have an on-call counselor available if you need to talk, or we're here to listen. Be more responsible, got it?"

Missy nodded.

"Go home and rest for tomorrow."

Echo waited for Missy in her car and didn't ask questions. They discussed the hike, and Echo mentioned swimming and her intolerance for the heat. She agreed and thanked Echo for the ride. Moom had dinner ready, but Missy wasn't hungry. She wrote in her journal and took a hot bath.

Her dreams jumped all over with Starr. *By chance was Jim Starr from the past? Was he reincarnated or was he another time traveler like Coach Bell believed in?* She needed serious help. She put in an extra squeeze of lavender bubble bath to soak in and lay back. Missy heard the toilet flush from the adjacent bathroom. Someone must have entered while the tub was being filled with water.

"You probably need to go home since your nightmares followed you here. I don't want to deal with them or you," Maura said, knocking on the wall.

"What? Your voice sounds mushy. Is your tongue tired of talking or kissing Brett too much?" She pulled the drain to cover any sounds from both sides of the wall. The only sound she heard was Maura's forceful door slam.

As Missy searched the tub for the washcloth, she saw the bubbles form into a sentence.

The time is near. Beware.

"How close is the time? What time?" She swished the bubbles to erase the message and got out. She needed to sleep and stop thinking. Too bad her mind was active in dreams.

***

Missy put on her hiking boots and walked to Jump Creek Canyon. She made it back to the lookout ridge by the Native American's face.

In the warm air, her thoughts were consumed by her feeling of being misunderstood. It wasn't just Maura anymore. Everyone was against her. Only Echo seemed to understand her.

She looked up at the mountainside. The scene repeated itself, reminding her of the previous mockery she endured. What does it have to say to her now?

She inquired, "Who are you, and why does the mountainside resemble you?"

"I'm Chief Tso'ape-ha. I'm here to protect you from the bad people."

"Who are the bad people?"

"I showed you the light in the tunnel to get you away from Jim. People have betrayed us. It must end." A tear formed and flowed out of his eye.

In her dream, Missy wiped at a tear that had formed in her eye. Despite facing opposition from almost everyone, how could she persist in unraveling this mystery?

She wiped the tears and opened her eyes.

This newfound knowledge brought her closer to the truth. The mountain was alive.

Chapter 17

Friday's practice was typical, but Maura seemed more likable. Reed wasn't there, which made Missy happy. He'd stress her out. When Echo questioned her about last night, she offered no response.

It was still early after dinner, and Missy needed some alone time. "Moom," she said to Mrs. Derringer, who was reading a book.

"Hmm?"

"Going for a walk. Won't be gone long."

"Okay."

Missy put on her jacket. Maura was doing schoolwork. "Meeting Reed?"

"No. Me time."

"Boring."

She eyed her and went outside. *Breathe in the good, exhale the bad. Fresh air, clean thoughts.* She intended to pet the horses but ended up by the Snake River. She watched the water flow downstream at a medium pace. There were smooth areas, others had small wakes. Nearby, a couple of large rocks sat in the river, partially submerged with water on their rough surfaces.

Missy likened her life to a river. "I have permanent unnoticed bruises from smashing into the rocks daily."

Trying to escape the harsh waves, she maneuvered through the cracks with difficulty. She wasn't the popular easily liked ones like Maura or Ally. Heck, she was a sidekick to fill in the blanks.

Brandon and Reed. Choices. Missy's vulnerability arose from her need for attention, popularity, and to be seen as fun. She took a couple of steps onto the bridge and hoped to see Starr out for his ride. She wondered if the face at Jump Creek was protecting his grave and if she'd see him riding far away from his burial place.

Missy laughed and envisioned Starr riding up and down the mountain's steep side. Not. Perhaps it was an ancient Native American ritual site, now requiring protection. But she remembered what Tso'ape-ha had said. He was watching over her.

Fortunately, the narrow bridge had side ropes to hold on to. Missy leisurely walked to the middle and glanced at the other side. A vision from her past resurfaced, and it wasn't a dream like she'd had last night.

Chief Tso'ape-ha was on the bridge. It wasn't a bright, cheerful glow. He lowered his head. "My soul is sad. History stays history and shouldn't be disturbed."

Suddenly, he disappeared.

It happened too fast for Missy to react. She looked around, searching for any sign of Tso'ape'ha's relocation, then turned back to the bridge's end, hoping to catch a glimpse of his return.

What did his words have to do with Starr, Brandon, or Jim? He had said Jim in her dream. She wondered if she needed to forget all three. Her life was confusing. She believed Brandon was history. But what would happen to Reed when she stopped living with Maura? Phone relationships weren't good, and she wouldn't drive to Murphy to see him. She doubted Reed would see her in

Nampa. He'd be too busy with the gym, making corn mazes, and chasing Starr.

"Nice evening for a walk."

Missy spun around with her hands up. "Stop startling me!"

"Okay, okay. I thought you heard me. I called out your name." He stepped back. "I came to see you, but Maura mentioned you've been gone for an hour."

Looking at the river, she felt vulnerable. "An hour? I barely left."

Reed moved behind Missy. She leaned her back on his chest, stopping her emotional battle, and gave the present time to Reed. "Do you believe in spirits?"

"Ghosts? You know I do. I'm the one who told you about Starr." His hands rubbed her arms. "And I wanted to see if you were okay since Thursday. I feel I've dragged you into a dark place you don't want, and I'm sorry. The whole thing is confusing, but I'm doing what my dad wants me to do. Follow Starr."

"To find what?"

"Here it is, and it sounds off the wall. There's a box, a treasure box, a chest buried with or by Starr, or so the family believes. It holds a connection to my mom's side of the family. There might be more than one."

"Boxes?"

Reed hunched. "My dad didn't fully tell his visions. It's believed Starr grabbed the piece of jewelry he gave the girl he fell in love with after killing her on the train. Next, he gave it to his wife, named Chaundra. She had a kid and left Starr. Dad wants to see if there's any connection or jewelry in a buried chest. Crazy, right?"

"No. At least you have a reason for the dreams. I don't."

"It would confuse me, too. I go along with the flow to help my parents out."

"Does your mom help look?"

"Oh, no! Dad puts his foot down. Doesn't want her to get hurt."

Missy nodded. "I believe ghosts are from evil people. Spirits are from good people." She moved to look at Reed. "The spirit can be a guardian. Lead you in a good way."

"Is this good spirit telling you to kiss me?" His thumb ran across her lips.

"No."

He pulled back.

"But my spirit says yes." It was nice, but the sound of a train stopped the kiss short.

"Stupid train." Reed grunted.

"I hope we get to see Starr." They crossed to the other side and stood by a big rock beside the tracks. "We'll stand here, safe from the train."

Neigh . . . The sudden sound pricked at her ears. "Are my ears playing tricks or did a horse whinny?" she asked. There it was again.

"You heard right." Reed smiled.

"What about the horse? Is it going to trample us?" Missy noticed there wasn't much room between the large rock and the train track.

"I'm a pro at doing this. We'll be fine."

Missy's feet vibrated like an earthquake as the train got closer. Her heart thumped. Whether it was excitement or fear, she did not know, only that she wanted to see Starr.

The train's headlights beamed around the corner, and its rays illuminated a fully dressed Native American alongside the train. Starr stopped twenty feet in front of them.

She gasped as the train thundered past, and Reed held her tight. The chief stared at them. His face was blank, registering neither surprise nor anger, but Missy felt calm. The prolonged stare left her unsure of how to react. Much to her surprise, Starr bowed his head, turned around, and galloped back.

"Oh, my heck, he stared right at us. What did he want? Was he going to hurt us?" She pulled on Reed's arm.

"Be calm. I'm not sure why Starr stopped, but it could've been because he saw me standing with a gorgeous girl." He hugged her.

"True," Missy said before heading back to the house.

"Where are you going?"

"My brain is drained. I've had enough excitement for one day."

"No more hugs?" Reed pouted.

Missy shrugged, "I guess so." She smiled and offered her share of the hug.

"That's more like it. 'Til we meet again."

She waved, got off the bridge, and watched Reed walk home. Once he was out of sight, Missy returned to the bridge and sat on the edge to clear her mind. Seeing both Chief Tso'ape'ha and Starr confirmed they weren't the same person.

It made her think about Brandon and Reed. She liked them both, but Brandon gave her an extra special feeling in her heart even though he'd dumped her and wouldn't be surprised if a new girl had stepped in her place. But now, she had to unravel her involvement in Murphy's peculiar occurrences.

Chapter 18

Jim and Dwight didn't make it back to Murphy until Saturday morning. Rock and Carlos came and helped reset the equipment at the car lot. They did a couple of test runs and got it set to perfection. They bagged a few pints, made sales, and got a list of customer names in Owyhee County. At 8:15 a.m., they were at BF Café.

"Who are we meeting?" Dwight stepped out of the car and opened the trunk.

"Two customers. They've purchased before—high school guys on a gymnastics team. Twist will help them be flexible." Jim smiled and sat on the hood of his car.

"A gymnastics team in *Ghost Town,* Murphy?"

"It's Idaho, so yeah."

An old Ford pickup truck entered and parked by Jim's car. The guy on the passenger side with short black hair got out. "Jim and Dwight?"

They both nodded.

"I'm Leo, and this is David." He handed Jim two hundred-dollar bills. "Even a small amount of Twist is better than none."

Dwight handed Leo a small bag. "Understand. We're close, so if you need more, here is our number." He gave Leo a plain business card with a number on it.

"Thanks. We'll be in contact often." Leo left.

"Must be gymnastics practice or a meet today. They may win or at least feel good about competing. It'd be nice if the coach saw the difference and used Twist as a medical need for his team. We'd be rich, rich, and rich. We'd take the money and move on before getting caught."

Dwight rubbed his hands together like a dog getting ready to bite a thick piece of raw steak. "I can feel it now."

Jim folded the money and put it in the front pocket of his jeans. The next stop was the cave.

Chapter 19

Reed pulled Missy aside after practice. "I want to show you a probable location."

"My parents are expecting me home." She raised her eyebrows.

"Use the phone in the office and let them know you'll be late or absent until tomorrow." He looked desperate.

"Fine." Lying was getting easier. She followed Reed to the office, called her parents, and said they had more optional practice for the gymnastic meet next week. She needed to work on her floor and beam routines. They understood and thanked her for the call.

Missy waited for Maura to leave before she went with Reed. To avoid Maura causing a fuss, any additional activities had to be kept secret. Reed seemed to understand.

"Where are we going?" Reed opened the truck door for Missy.

"There's a popular area by the train track and mountains. I haven't hiked in certain areas for months, but I want to revisit them."

To kill time, Missy inquired about Reed's wildest river experiences. He recounted the river challenge he and his junior high friends had, trying to take as many steps as possible before submerging. He pulled into the same place Missy had played hooky. They got out of the truck.

"Reed?"

"Yes." He put his hand on her arm.

"I'm puzzled. You can do this yourself. Why wait to do it with me? Your dad advised against going near the train tracks, the forest, and river trails day or night."

"He's more concerned about safety," Reed answered, "hurting your muscles from tripping and falling—from you especially." He smiled.

She disliked the idea of anyone knowing she was clumsy.

"But it's true," Reed continued, still smirking a little. "I'm not being hurtful in saying it. Everyone has a glitch of imperfection."

"And yours is a control problem."

Reed was silent.

"Why are you taking me instead of going alone?"

They walked for a couple of minutes before he answered her, though not directly. "The river is rapid and has a powerful undercurrent."

"It sounds like he's hiding a secret and doesn't want to scare everyone away with Starr." Missy stopped walking.

"True. I believe Dad has had more personal visits than anyone. He doesn't want us in danger." Reed scanned the side of the mountain, searching for a trail. "And I wanted to include you." He turned to face her. "You seem to understand why I'm doing this."

"I do. We both have secrets." She sensed his desire to kiss her once more. The feeling was swimming all around her. "Have you seen him lately?" She walked a few steps ahead of him.

"Did you forget we both saw him? Plus, I have once in Silver City."

Missy continued her walk up the trail.

"Stop. Here's the place to climb." Reed waved her back. The indents are large enough to fit your foot into. It's about ten feet up."

She climbed and stood by the tree she had sat by on her last visit. "Now what?"

Reed glanced over the area and found the overgrown, hidden trail. "I can see someone's been up here recently."

She shrugged. She didn't want Reed to know it was likely her footprints there. Undeterred by her previous encounter, she bravely ducked under the same branch.

Reed was a couple of feet behind her. "You must have great eyesight knowing where to bend and put your feet."

"Pure luck." They reached the side of the mountain, and Missy touched the cross. "Did Sky die here?"

Reed felt around the hand-crafted holes. "Nobody knows. Since they only found one of his belongings here, they deemed it the best place for the cross."

"Any openings on the mountain? This was never finished. Only a few holes."

"I hope so. Maybe it's where Sky died." Reed peaked into one hole. "It looks like there is an opening. The entrance might be blocked by trees on that side." He coughed. "Need fresh air." He walked back to her. "Do you smell the odor?"

"I do, and it's making me lightheaded. I'm out of here." She walked back down the mountain trail to Reed's truck.

Reed followed and kept his arms to himself. "You okay?"

"I'm having problems sleeping. Too much on my mind." She rubbed her eyes. "Too many decisions to make. Should I, shouldn't I? I wish I had, I wish I hadn't, you know." Missy opened her mouth to say more, but Reed's hand covered it.

"Hey there. Hush-hush. Rest your mouth, and let's get you home. It's okay. We'll go another time and climb higher. Nevertheless, the smell must be examined."

She didn't like what he said, hated being controlled, and didn't say goodbye when he dropped her off by her car.

Half aware of her surroundings and bewildered, Missy drove home. She felt off balance with a negative feeling. She changed the radio station. *"You're messing with secrets,"* the music blared. She pulled over and parked on the roadside.

There it was again. The warning. What was the secret and who kept it hidden? Reed? His dad? She didn't know.

Missy didn't realize she had pulled into her driveway until she was there. She was numb. She grabbed her belongings, went inside the front door, and smelled dinner cooking. "Hi." Emotions hit her like lightning.

Her mom put down a glass, reached her halfway, and hugged her. Missy burst into tears. "Sweetie, you're upset." She escorted her to the couch in the front room. "Ray, will you please turn off the stove?"

"Yes, dear." He came to hug her, but her mom's nod told him they needed time alone.

Missy sat, leaned her head on her mom's shoulder, and cried her heart out. "I don't know what's wrong. I can't say. Not sleeping, tired. I'm so stressed, Mom. And I'm having bad dreams. *Bad . . . dreams.*" Her words barely made a sound as she whispered.

"Oh, honey, let it all out. You'll feel better afterward." She paused for a moment before continuing. "Did I tell you about a high school test I had to take my senior year? I was shy but smart in school. I felt pressured to keep my grades up. Tests were hard for me. I studied day and night to make sure I'd pass."

She looked at her mom. "You were under pressure as a teen?" Of course. A smart student and I were striving for the top grade in the same class. I wanted to prove I was smarter because, in this class, I was always second best. Anyway, I didn't get enough sleep because I overstudied, but what made it worse was I studied the wrong questions. I paid no attention to the teacher's guidance. I got a C on the test and the stress was so intense, I thought I might have a heart attack. It affected my attitude and sleep."

She massaged Missy's back. "I look back and laugh at my overreaction, but it was still difficult. Even now things get hard."

"As an adult?"

"Of course."

She was relieved her mom had had hard times in her life and understood. Getting a good grade on a test wasn't as challenging as her current situation though, it seemed. She was hearing voices and having dreams and trying to live a normal life as a gymnast. How does that compare to test preparation?

"This Saturday, we're competing against a tough team, and I feel pressured," Missy explained. "We are pushed so hard to do our routines perfect and required to make them smooth—non-mechanical. That's the hardest part."

"I understand. Things pile up, like a tall stack of laundry," her mom said.

She gave her mom one last squeeze and found her dad at the table reading the newspaper.

"Hi, Dad. Sorry for the crying."

"A cry does us good. Did you know us dads cry, too?"

"I'm sure it's rare." She chuckled.

After dinner, Missy spent the rest of the night on her bed, reading, and writing in her journal. The thought of calling Julie made her more exhausted and wished she had a calm sleeping night. Boy was her wish wrong. Brandon and Reed haunted her dreams.

The dream began with Brandon watching her kissing Reed on the train track in Murphy, and she told him they were done. But in the next part, she kissed Brandon with Reed watching, and they get into a fight.

"No. Stop it."

"We both want the hidden treasure," Reed said.

The dream changed to the field across the street from where she lived, with Brandon and Reed driving a tractor.

"No!" she yelled at Reed. "You don't deserve it." She moved over by Brandon's tractor. "Why are we digging holes in the field?" She climbed the side of the tractor to sit by him on the one-person seat.

"We're looking for the tunnel where the hidden treasures are."

"We found it last year."

"I know. There is another coffin full of money." Brandon kept driving to different spots to dig new holes. As he neared the pit's edge, he noticed Reed doing the same in his tractor.

"Hey, you two, go away. The treasure's mine." Reed lifted the metal beast digger as it roared and drove full force toward her and Brandon.

The pit was inches away from them both when she woke up from her dream and shivered. She grabbed her pillow and banged it on the bed several times to get her anger out. She didn't need these dreams.

Chapter 20

The life of living with the Derringers and visiting home blurred into one big blob. Time blinked. The gymnastics meet two weeks past was a piece of crap for Missy. Lack of sleep, excessive homework, and venturing into forbidden hiking spots all contributed to her ranking outside the top four. When she did go home to visit, she isolated herself in her bedroom so she wouldn't accidentally run into Brandon, though she was pretty sure he'd forgotten about her by now.

Missy felt the week of hard practice didn't do justice on Friday's practice. She kept messing up the floor routine, and she came close to twisting her ankle again for the thousandth time. In a semi-nice, aggravated way, Coach Kirk told her to 'pay attention.'

She headed to the foyer for a drink when Reed arrived from the parking lot. He checked her out. "Not having a good day?"

"You can tell?" She snatched a towel and blotted her face, wiping the sweat off.

"Your expression."

She tossed the towel in the hamper. "Problems sleeping." She felt like she was standing on a tightrope, unbalanced. She was ready to fall, uncertain of who would be there to catch her.

Reed stepped closer and hugged her. "Pre-competition nerves. I had them when I was on the team." He gave her a one-arm squeeze. "You'll do fine."

"I should go back inside to avoid your dad's wrath."

"My dad, you're fine. It's Hopkins I don't like. He's one reason I left."

Missy gave a questioning look. Another hidden mystery that's better to stay buried. She believed Kirk was the nicer of the two.

"Not here or now to talk." He glanced in the gym. "Step inside; let me see if I can offer any help. What routine are you having trouble with?"

"All." With hands on hips, she marched into the gym, followed by Reed.

"Okay."

Maura finished a floor routine as Missy headed to the beam. Panting, she paraded over and nudged Missy's shoulder. "Did you see? I did it. I did my double twist and kept my feet cemented on my landing."

"No. But I saw your feet touch the floor. Nice."

She yanked Missy's braid. "What's with you?"

Missy flapped her arms. "Ugh. I can't talk about it. You wouldn't understand." In frustration, she stomped to the foyer and exited through the front door. To drown out the pain, she spun in a circle.

Reed came out carrying her sweats. She snatched them and put them on. "Lack of sleep does affect your attitude."

"Not nice," she snapped back.

He raised his arms. "If looks could kill."

She took his hand briefly. "Sorry. Forgive me?"

"Your face makes it impossible for me not to forgive you."

That melted the ice.

He planted a quick kiss on her lips. "If you don't go back in, we'll be in trouble."

The quick kiss broke through her negative thoughts. Her goal was to beat Maura. If not in all routines, the floor and beam were top priorities. She had to prove to herself she was better than Maura.

Missy gulped a drink from her water bottle and headed back to the gym. Her timely entrance was exactly what she needed to witness. Maura did her dismount off the beam and fell. She tried hard not to smile. "Nice try, M."

"Let's see you do it," she grunted.

"No, thanks." Missy stretched her legs out. "I'll stick to mine."

"Yours is harder. Why'd you pick it?" Maura asked.

"I like the challenge."

Coach Kirk placed the jump board by the beams. "Back to Earth?"

"Yes. Sorry." Missy squinched her face.

He smiled. "All energy goes into the routines. Let's see you show it." He straightened the mat at the end of the beam. "You're set."

The beam was Missy's weakest area, and she said a quick, silent prayer and wiped her hands on a towel. She saluted and Coach Kirk okayed her to start. Missy jumped onto the beam, did the Chinese splits perfectly and moved her upper body to the side splits.

"Nice." Coach Kirk did a single clap.

Up on her feet, she made ballet moves with twists and leaps. Her last stunt before dismounting made her nervous. Missy prayed her hair was pinned tight enough not to loosen and cause a fall. She did not want to repeat it like a month ago. Roundoff, backflip. Turn halfway, cartwheel, and double backflip dismount. Perfect landing.

"You did it!" Echo ran and hugged her. The coaches clapped.

Staci said, "Good job. You make it look easy."

"Thank you."

Reed handed a water bottle to Missy. "Beautiful. I'd kiss you if we didn't have an audience." He laughed. "Don't worry. My dad likes you."

Her cheeks burned. *Wonderful. Not.*

Echo pulled her away from Reed. He's really into you. So lucky."

"It's not how it looks."

"I don't care. I'm jealous," Echo admitted.

"Please don't be. You can find better guys on the team or elsewhere. Trust me. There's more to a person than their looks."

She shrugged. "I'd like to hang out sometime besides practice. I think we could have fun."

Missy agreed to set up a time soon, but mentally, she was sure it wouldn't happen. Throughout the evening, Maura pestered Missy about the seriousness of her relationship with Reed. Then she put a guilt trip on Missy and hoped her luck on beam carried on to competition.

She felt more pressure having her parents come to watch after she begged and begged and told them she wasn't ready for them to come tomorrow. Bending Julie's arms a few times was hard enough because she was not in the mood to handle observers.

***

Saturday morning was terrible. Missy slept in, and it put Maura in a rant. It put pressure on Missy, and she messed up during the competition. She fell off the beam twice, lost her grip on the bars, but caught it before landing on the floor. On her floor routine, her aerial ended up being a one-handed cartwheel. Crappy. It reminded her of a beginner back in junior high.

After the meet, Missy swallowed her pride and faced Maura back home who got second place overall. But to her surprise, Maura kept to herself as well.

Missy's parents knew she was staying over the weekend because of the activities and would see her Monday morning before dropping off her homework at Nampa High.

The Derringers went to a friend's house for a fun Halloween night with Maura's little brother, Jack. Sandy went to her own friend's house to watch movies.

Missy hoped the night would be fun enough to enjoy herself and erase the morning blues. She showered and dressed in faded jeans with a long-sleeved padded button shirt with the sleeves rolled up to her elbows. She styled her hair in two braids.

To kill time, she spread cream cheese on a bagel. Maura walked into the kitchen wearing only jeans and a bra. She remained silent, assuming Maura would retrieve her shirt from the laundry room.

Maura copied Missy, opting for strawberry jam on her bagel. "Excited for tonight? Is Reed picking you up? What time?"

"Yes, at six-thirty. What are your plans with Brett?"

Maura smiled. "He wants me to meet his parents. They only live a fifteen-minute drive from here, so we'll go before dinner. He'll arrive in 30 minutes." Maura chewed her bagel and looked out the window. "The mail came." She walked out the door shirtless.

Missy watched Maura walk outside with only a bra on. Still, it was pretty funny. She walked to the front porch. "Um, Maura. What color is your shirt?" she asked.

Maura looked down and curled over. "Oh, my gosh!" She hurriedly returned to her room in the house.

Brett came and got Maura at 5:30 p.m., right on time. Reed arrived at six thirty in his dad's old Ford truck. He wore Wrangler jeans, a plaid button shirt, and cowboy boots.

"Howdy there, ma'am," Reed said with a southern drawl. He took off his cowboy hat and bowed.

She laughed. "Howdy back there, sir." She bowed back. "Ready to do hick town square dancing?"

"You got it right, and we can't be whole until you wear this." He had another cowboy hat and placed it on her head.

"Yee-haw, I'm hungry. Watch out, Murphy. Here comes Missy with an attitude."

They arrived at the Grange building and parked on the side. Behind the building was a big field with a covered picnic area. They crammed a long table on the side with salads, rolls, veggies, fruit, desserts, and drinks. The smell of barbecued chicken floated their way.

Echo called out to Missy and waved her hands to invite her to sit with her and Rich. "Where's Maura and Brett?"

Gwynn showed up and sat by her. "Hi. Boy, the food smells good."

"I agree." She looked back at Echo. "Brett wanted to introduce Maura to his parents. They should be back soon." She shrugged.

A few snickered. Gwynn continued, "It's Brett's gig with every girl he meets. He wants them to feel like he's all over them and can't live without them. He plays around, gets bored, and moves on in the long run." Maura and Brett were getting out of his car. "I know because I was a victim."

"I'm so sorry," Echo said.

"Don't worry. I didn't like Brett past a friend. As a newcomer, he aimed to treat me like royalty. Since Maura's new in town, she will receive a tour of hidden spots before breaking up and being single."

Missy tried hard not to smile. If Maura took charge and plans failed, she would end things with Brett.

Maura and Brett filled their plates and joined their group at the table. "Hi, people. Enjoying yourselves?" Maura asked. They squeezed into the small space across from Missy and sat down.

"Hi there," Echo said. "You're in time for the first round of square dancing. They're setting up the speakers."

"The last time I square danced was in P.E. two years ago. Do-si-dos and bows to your partner. Kick your heels up and step to your right," Missy bantered in an accent. They laughed.

"You should be the caller." Reed raised his eyebrows.

Once the teammates finished their seconds and desserts, the announcer instructed everyone to form groups of eight and create squares. Older couples formed their squares, and it encouraged others to participate. Reed dragged Missy out to finish off a square. They danced for half an hour, and she learned how to line dance.

Tony, in her gymnastics group, tapped Missy's back as she was leaving the dance area. "Can I have the next dance?"

She smiled. "Sure. Let's boogie the night away."

After a few fast songs, slow music played. "Can I sneak in one more?"

"Glad it's a slow one. I'm not sure I can boogie again."

Tony continued the conversation. "I heard you like to fish. You don't get grossed out by cleaning them?"

She giggled. "Nope. It's cool in a morbid way. I've never been hunting, so cutting deer or elk might be different. But I won't know until I try, right?"

The song ended. "When you're available, call me, and I'll take you to a great fishing area."

"Sure." *I doubt it will ever happen.* "Thanks."

Reed wanted to go into the corn maze with the dance in full swing. Missy agreed and walked the short distance to the entrance. "Want to split and see who reaches the exit first?" Reed asked.

"I might get lost or encounter a dragon. Or maybe witches will fly over the field, cursing people with their wands."

"If a witch was flying, I'd want to see if she gave free rides. Doesn't it sound fun riding on a broomstick?"

"Only if it has a thick padded seat, so I'd prefer to go together. I'm unfamiliar with this place, and I'm sure you know the maze with your eyes closed. Does the maze stay the same?"

"It's a different pattern every year. I've helped plan the maze so, yes, I can go through it with my eyes closed." He lifted his shoulders like it wasn't a big deal.

"Lead the way, trailblazer, and no getting lost on purpose. Remember my warning on Monday about my feet?"

"Oh, ho, ho. My word is my honor. No neck biting tonight. You have a competition soon and need all your blood." He gave her a reassuring look. "Trust me?"

"If I see an actual witch flying, I'll flag her down for a potential escape."

Reed entered the maze, and Missy followed. Their feet crunched on the broken-up cornhusks. Not far in, she swore she heard a voice beside her. She stopped to listen.

Stay away.

She spun around and peered through the stalks on either side. Nobody. *You're in a corn maze. Be calm.* She shook her head to clear her mind.

Reed came back around a corner. "Hey, why did you stop? I was talking to myself and not knowing it." He gestured with his hand. "Come on."

"My shoe. I had to tie my shoe."

They walked in circles, growing smaller and smaller until they arrived in the middle of the cornfield in an open area. Others searched for the proper exit to leave.

"We circled around and returned to this spot. Let's go this way." An older couple walked to a different exit.

"Are they suggesting they arrived here like us, found another route, and ended up back here again?" Missy asked.

"It's a maze. Getting lost and not knowing the way out is normal. Don't worry. The remaining will be guided out at night's end. Look closely at the rows when you walk. There is one straight exit out of the corn maze. It's the one we'll go out."

They chose one of six exits and walked straight out of the field, moving cornstalks to reveal the trail. Reed and his partners did a great job designing the maze.

Reed escorted Missy home after the corn maze and a few dances, expressing gratitude for the enjoyable evening. "I'll pick you up early in the morning for another hike. It's an area I haven't checked out yet, and I want you to experience it with me."

"It may be dangerous."

"Perhaps, but I must find answers." He placed his hand on her cheek.

"I'm as ready as you are. Good night." She turned and left. Feeling uneasy, she lay on the bed and stared at the ceiling before going to sleep. It was as if Jim and Starr shared a sinister laugh as they devised the perfect plan to ruin her life.

Without knocking, Maura walked into the room. "Did you have fun tonight with Reed?" She sat on the bed.

Missy pulled a strand of hay standing out from Maura's hair. "I can see you had fun. If I may ask, what did you do?"

"First, why didn't you stay to go into the haunted house? The young kids weren't scared walking through the so called haunted barn. Brett and I went twice to try and scare anyone. On our second attempt, we stumbled upon a back door to the barn, next to some hay bales. Need I say more?"

"Um, I hope you don't get hurt in the long run."

"It won't happen. I've heard the whole story plenty of times. If he backs off, I'm the one who will push him away. And for the record, we were helping the farmer move the hay bales. Hahaha. Got you thinking, didn't I?" She halfheartedly pushed Missy's arm and laughed. "Maybe a few minutes alone in the hay though." She cleared her throat. "So, what did you and Reed do?" She peeked at Missy's neck.

"Should I undress so you can check for any additional marks or hickeys on my body? No, no hickeys. Make you happy?" She scowled.

"Jeez, girl, what's your problem?" Maura asked.

"You wouldn't understand."

Maura exhaled, ran her hand through her hair, and sat back. "How long have we known each other?"

Was she claiming they were always best friends, despite it not being true? She frowned. "Since we were five years old. Why?"

"I've never known your middle name," Maura admitted.

"What?"

"I don't know your middle name. You know mine."

"True. It's Lynne." She pointed at Maura.

"So?" Maura prompted.

"So, what?"

"Stop it."

"Fine. It's Violet," Missy stated.

"Your mom's name. I should've known. Missy Vie will be your new name."

She tossed a pillow at Maura. "I say no."

Maura caught the pillow and swung it back for defense as Missy flung hers to the side and hit Maura's shoulder. She, in return, pushed it on Missy's face. They fell off the bed and laughed until they cried.

Missy remembered the old times. It was all about pillow fights and feet tickle attacks—simple grade-school fun until Ally took her place with Maura.

Chapter 21

Nine in the morning, Reed picked up Missy and drove to a new area with a view of the mountains and river. He ventured off the old dirt trail and onto the forbidden train track for a new walk.

"Um, why are we doing this?" Missy hoped a train wasn't scheduled soon.

"I told you. We're searching for Starr's grave."

"I've seen no signs of anything close, and we'll be late getting back home before dark."

"It's only eleven. We've got hours of sun."

"It's fall. The day doesn't stay sunny long." She looked straight ahead and hoped their hike would end soon. Ten minutes of silence went by with no sight of caves, graves, or abnormal figures.

"I'm thirsty. Didn't make a smart decision coming with nothing to eat or drink."

"You can be a pest. Don't you see I have a backpack on?" Reed shook his body to make the pack move.

Missy hit her forehead with her palm. "Stupid me for not noticing it. It's brown like your shirt."

Reed shrugged and got out two water bottles. "Guess I'm a little thirsty, too. Sorry for not telling you the full details of this trip. I didn't want you to say no." He stepped close to her. "Forgive me?"

She drank the last drop of water and shoved it back into his pack.

"I told my dad where we were going, and he was okay with it."

"I thought he'd want us to stay away. Far, far away."

"A long walk for sure. You okay?"

"Fine, stop talking, so I don't have to look at you."

After another fifteen minutes of walking, the hill got steeper. "This is the trail to Silver City," Reed said. An indentation caught their attention on the right side of the mountain. There was a cave entrance. "Well, lookie here. We found a cave." He stepped off the track. "And no river to cross." He hiked to the opening a good thirty yards away.

She wasn't far behind him. "Is this a smart move?" Her gut got queasy as she looked around. "And see?" She pointed to the top of the hill by the cave. "We could've driven a lot closer."

He saw where she was pointing. "I wasn't sure if we could drive close to the trail. I'll look. Stay put."

Missy waited for Reed, who returned within a minute.

"I'll drive and look for the cut-off on the main road to Silver City." An old car sat in a parking spot beyond the ridge. "It might be a local or a drifter."

"Got it."

Reed walked close to Missy and took off his backpack. "Perfect spot for our picnic." He unloaded items, including a small blanket to sit on and two paper bags of food. "Here, sit and enjoy a homemade lunch. It took me hours to make it."

"For sure."

She pulled out a peanut butter and jelly sandwich, a plastic bag with celery, carrots, and an apple. Her feet throbbed and sitting sounded good. She took the food bag with another water bottle and peeked in it. She laughed. It reminded her of her mom sending her a lunch bag in elementary school.

"It's a healthy lunch with all the important vitamins and minerals to keep your body perfect before the next competition." Reed sniggered.

"Okay."

"Do you know how to ride horses?" Reed asked unexpectedly.

"Yes. My friends have horses, and I took lessons." Missy chuckled. "The owners of the horse I learned to ride on named him, Me Too." She chewed on a piece of the apple. "The instructor noted that Me Too would trot along behind whenever any of the other horses were allowed to leave. That is how he got his name."

"Horse with an attitude, but no horse beats Ted."

"Ted? A brother I don't know about?"

"If our horse was a human, he'd be easier to discipline. Ted was a naughty horse." Reed leaned back on his elbows and stretched his legs out. "He kept running away."

"How can a horse run away?" *Well, yeah, not tied or an open gate, I suppose.*

"Whenever I went to feed them, he was never around, so I'd hop in the truck and search for him. Ted would be in a different field eating away. I'd have to rope him and pull him back to the barn. He wasn't happy."

"Sounds like my brother." She chuckled, recalling Tommy's dash across the street to the shed where he encountered Jim, the ghost driving the tractor.

"We never figured out how Ted got out until I caught him in action. The horse knew our schedule, so he knew when to sneak off. Well, he was wrong one day. I left for work a bit earlier and caught sight of Ted crawling under the fence while passing the field. Hearing the truck, he swiftly turned, crawled back under, and rushed to the barn."

"Are you serious? Your horse could crawl under the fence rail?"

"I'm serious. Never seen anything like it. Ted was a flexible retired show horse."

"Do you still have Ted?"

"No. He got sick a year ago, and we put him to sleep. It was sad. Instead of a horse, he seemed more like a troublesome little brother." Reed stood and gathered his trash. Missy followed suit.

"Now it's time for action." He got his flashlight out of his pack and walked to the cave's entrance.

"I don't feel comfortable doing this. What if gang members are inside? Nobody knows where we are."

"Mellow. My dad knows where to look. Be quiet and don't trip or start an avalanche."

Missy got tired of being treated like a stupid klutz. He wasn't the same person when she'd met him either. She stopped, and Reed lost his balance holding her arm to keep her from stumbling.

"Why'd you stop? You almost caused me to fall."

"Too bad it didn't happen. I guess I'm not the only klutz."

He eyed her strangely.

"I'm tired of being used and pushed around like a wet sponge. I've recently learned to stick up for myself, and I'm doing it."

"What are you talking about? I'm not pushing you around, am I?"

"You treat me like a stupid kid. I've been tripping and hurting my ankle for the past couple of months. Did you know I have a stress fracture, and it gives out? I push myself to be equal to or surpass everyone else. Being treated like a dumb child won't be helpful, you know? What do you want from me, anyway, besides harassing me? Am I your kissy toy when you feel like it? I'm not the same person anymore."

Reed was silent as the sound of rocks hitting the ground echoed from the cave. Reed put on his backpack, ready to go. "I bet we disturbed the resting spirits."

"No. You dragged me here, and if I get attacked by aliens, I don't care. I want to see what's inside. Maybe there's a coffin. Aren't you curious?"

Reed's expression showed he knew what was there. "Okay, but let me go first."

"Aye-aye, Captain. Whatever floats your boat."

"You have an attitude."

"Deal with it," Missy snapped.

Another rock hit the ground. Reed put his hand up to stop her from getting closer. He stepped up to a bigger opening, peered around the corner and cleared his throat as if he'd inhaled dust. He moved his arm to gesture Missy to come and look.

A bit nervous, she crossed her fingers. Dead bodies wouldn't be hanging on a rope or lying on the ground, would they? She closed her eyes, turned the corner, and opened them to get it over with. *Hallelujah! No dead bodies.* The only things she saw were two big conveyor belts like a soldering machine, but instead of soldering electronic boards, the heat dried up the herbs. "I don't—" She looked in surprise as two belts slowly moved the herbs to dry and dropped them off into a big canister.

A rock flew across the opening.

Reed covered her mouth and whispered, "I believe whoever's here wants us to leave."

She glanced around once more and spotted a partially buried chest, roughly the size of three shoe boxes, at the side of the room. She pointed toward it.

Reed tilted his head toward the exit and suggested they needed to leave.

Back on the trail, she exploded. "Did you see that? Is that Starr's? Are the treasures in the cave and it's the half-buried box what your dad wants? Is this what we've been searching for? Why are we leaving it there? And the machines were running. That's how they make Twist. I bet you it is."

"Calm down. I'll have my dad come and get it."

"Are you telling me to relax? You need to mellow, too."

Reed flared his nostrils. "I'm fighting my feelings because I like you and am too scared to show it." He turned to look at her. "I'm sorry for being arrogant."

She sneered back. "How is it relevant to getting the box? Why did you pull me away?"

He went on talking. "It's not time to get it. Besides, don't you want to get the guys who are doing this? If it's Starr's box, there's something Starr wants my mom to have. My dad feels the spirits will curse him for disturbing the box. The spirits prefer not to be bothered. I'll let him deal with it."

Another stone landed at their feet.

"Maybe you're right. Let's go." A slight chill caressed Missy's back and she had to agree. Buried history held secrets deemed unworthy of the time and effort to uncover. They were better off not knowing.

"What if Starr is buried there and guarded by real Native Americans?" she asked. "They're still here, and there's a possibility he has more undisclosed family." *Like Sky, Echo, and Vallie.* She touched Reed's back.

"We thought it was possible, though we haven't found medical paperwork or genealogy stating otherwise. It could be from any tribe guarding the cave."

"You going to tell your dad about the box?" Missy Asked.

"Yes."

"Last question. If you find an arrowhead, shouldn't you leave it there and not touch it? Isn't it a special place for it to stay?"

"I had the same question, but I discovered that finding an arrowhead while standing brings protection and blessings. Why?"

"Curious. I have two in my collection." *I don't need another curse on me.*

Chapter 22

Dwight closed a dozen plastic pint bags of Twist. "Will we see ghosts, ah, I mean Halloween spirits tonight?" He placed the bags in a box, exchanging them for empty ones as dust fell from the cave ceiling. "Will the cave fall in on us?"

"No. Probably a deer crossing over."

Jim sniffed a handful of Twist from a new batch. "There's a new contract in Grandview. Small towns are better than big cities. I see the pot of gold at the end of the rainbow." The men continued making Twist.

They heard voices from the entrance. "Doesn't sound like a deer to me. Rock said we'd be safe." Dwight wiped the sweat off his forehead.

"I'd die if it was Missy from Nampa again. She's always in the way."

"Your high school girlfriend's daughter, right?"

"Let's never mention that item again."

"Why?"

"Because the girl isn't Vivi." Jim threw rocks into the opening of the cave.

"We need to be quiet."

"Scares any intruders away, including ghosts." Jim knew it was a stupid reply but didn't care. Someone cleared their throat at the main entrance and interrupted his thoughts. "Sounds like Reed," he said, rising and heading toward the sleeping area entrance. Spotting Reed, he gestured for them to stay hidden for a moment by making an all-okay sign with his hand.

He came back to his spot and sat. "Reed found us and made sure we were okay. I trust the guy." Jim sniffed more Twist.

"I hope you're right." Dwight copied Jim.

Chapter 23

Missy kept to herself until they reached Reed's truck. "Ice cream sounds good." Reed unlocked the doors.

The bottoms of her feet throbbed worse after their lunch break, and she was exhausted. But ice cream sounded good. "Okay."

"There's a great place near BF Café called Simply Made." After driving for a few minutes, they arrived at the shop. "Contrary to belief, people do visit this place. Their ice cream is homemade from vanilla to chocolate, and wait until you try their blueberry/raspberry. Hmmm! Delicious."

Reed held the door open for Missy, and they sat at the bar on tall stools. The decorations reflected the 1950s era. She liked it. The place had a jukebox, and Elvis Presley's *Love Me Tender* filled the room.

"The day's flavors are on the chalkboard above the chef's window." Reed waved his hand at the sign.

She noticed and decided to try a new combination. Hazelnuts covered with chocolate in vanilla ice cream. "I'll take the special in a waffle cone."

"I'll do the same." He leaned over the counter. "Tricia, we're ready."

A young lady emerged from the store's rear. "Hello, Reed. What's going on?" She gave him a tight hug. "Who's your partner in crime today?"

"This is Missy. She's on Dad's gymnastics team and does a great job." He put his arm around her. Tricia seemed youthful, barely older than Reed, a seventeen-year-old.

"Nice to meet you. I'm Tricia, Reed's sister-in-law. I'm married to his older brother, Randy." With a mischievous smile, she appeared to know exactly what Missy was thinking.

She was right. "Hi, and nice to meet you, too," Missy said. She didn't know what else to say, so she watched Tricia make their ice cream cones.

She finished one and handed it to her. "Tell me if you like it."

Missy rotated the cone to ensure her tongue got a generous portion. "I'm in, like, ice cream heaven. I've never tasted ice cream this good before."

Tricia extended her arm toward the ceiling. "Hurrah! So glad you like it. Even if I make this type tomorrow, it won't be the same. Homemade always has a distinct flavor."

"Don't get me tempted to try your new flavor every day. I have a gymnast body to take care of."

"It would take a year of daily ice cream to make a difference." She washed her hands in the sink by the ice cream freezer. "Got to get back to work. Hope to see you around, Missy. Take care, Reed." She winked and went to the store's back.

"She's nice. Do they have any kids?"

"They have an eight-month-old baby girl. She probably went to the back for mom duties or to put the baby to sleep."

"Does she have a name?"

"After my mom. Chaundra Louise Bell. Tricia, the first daughter-in-law, will continue the family name since my mom had no daughters. It's a tradition." Reed wiped a drip of ice cream on the table with his finger and rubbed it on his pants. "The buried box might hold a clue, whether it's the one we saw or another. It's the other reason I'm trying to find it, to get information to answer a lot of whys."

"Well, it was there in plain sight. Picking it up was all we needed to do." Another oldie song played.

He offered his hand to Missy. "Want to dance?" It was obvious Reed had changed the subject. Granting him access, she glanced around as if the place was packed. "Come on. We're the only two here."

She accepted his hand and danced a slow song. The sound of a car door shutting made her pull away. She felt uncomfortable and out of place. "I need to go." She thanked Tricia again for the yummy ice cream. Missy saw a confused look on Reed's expression. It felt like she was cheating on Brandon. It made her feel sick.

In the truck, Reed reached for her hand across the seat as he drove. "Thanks for coming with me. The cave is a great spot to visit, but my dad and a few others will handle the box. Don't you think?"

He waited for her response, but her mind was consumed by his hand on hers.

They pulled into the driveway. "We might find some answers," he added, removing his hand and putting the car in park.

"Thanks for the ice cream. Yes, it was an interesting day." She smiled. "I'll see you tomorrow at practice."

She still felt uncomfortable, and she wanted to reply to his question, but something kept her from answering. Did she want others to help? Would that be the best move? She didn't think it was from the dance or his hand on hers. Despite the difficulty, she walked to the front door without glancing back.

Missy sat on the bed, marked the cave's location on her map, and tapped the pen on her leg. The cave they had left earlier felt like it held the answers because of the box and the drug making machines.

She felt antsy. A hot bath sounded good, but she didn't have the time. She snatched her keys and hugged Mrs. Derringer. "I'm off to my house for the night."

"Do you miss not being at your home, your bed?"

"Yes and no," she replied, reluctant to divulge any further information. Her negative attitude was getting worse, and she wasn't sure what to do. She loved gymnastics but not the challenging daily workouts and the pressure of doing her best and being more recognized than other teammates. She knew it sounded big-headed, but she wanted to stand out, too.

Missy pulled into her driveway and wondered if she could deal with her life. Would she strive to become a better gymnast and join a superior team, or long for her previous simple, happy life? No answer followed her questions, so she went inside. "Your only daughter is home!"

Her mom greeted her with a hug. "I had a feeling to make your favorite. Chicken, rice, and Jell-O."

"I can smell it. I miss my bed and family, even if it's a short drive away." Missy went to her room and dropped the duffle bag on the floor. She wasn't sure if she should call Julie or surprise her by going to her house after dinner.

She ended up calling Julie. "Hi, it's me. What are you doing on a boring Sunday night? Still have lots of homework to do?"

"No, no homework. I'm chilling. I went horse riding today with Gabe Stark, the guy who lives in the neighborhood a couple of miles from ours?"

"Going for the 4-H guys now?"

"Well, since my best friend has taken her life elsewhere, I must keep myself entertained. They live on a big farm, and his dad breeds and raises horses. I ride mine over and help him exercise theirs. It's a lot of fun. His parents are nice." Missy heard the excitement in Julie's voice.

"So, you're telling me you're falling in love, thanks to me leaving you space. Not sure if I feel hurt, deprived, or neglected." She frowned even though Julie couldn't see her. Mom knocked on the door, telling her it was time for dinner. "I got to go, but I want to hear full details when I see you soon."

After dinner, Missy helped her mom wash the dishes and ran to Julie's house.

"Hey, Julie. Now I have time to talk. Do you?"

Julie leaped forward and gave her a bear hug. She wasn't sure why she was so emotional lately. "I'm so happy to see you. I hate phone conversations. Come on. We still have leftover Halloween candy to snack on, and we can go talk in my room." Julie dumped candy into a bowl. "I miss our old times when we were inseparable."

They reached Julie's room, shut the door, and sat cross-legged on her bed.

"How did you meet Gabe? You're not one to go after the popular ones." Missy helped herself to a piece of candy.

"It was so weird. I went to the farm store to find a new brush for my horse and, coincidentally, Gabe was there in the same aisle searching for one, too. He asked what brand I liked, and I told him the one I used. Gabe thanked me, and turned to leave, but stopped." Red patches brightened on Julie's neck. She was excited. "He asked if my name was Julie. I said yes. He said, 'It's lunch, and I have free time. Want to join me at Dairy King?'"

"Oh, my gosh! Are you serious? Out of nowhere, he asked you out?" She got excited for Julie, too.

"I know, right? I said, 'Sure, let's go.' We drove there, and Gabe bought me lunch. Turns out we had a lot in common. He lives close by, and we are now horseback riding partners."

Missy seized her hands. "It sounds so romantic I can't stand it. I'm so happy for you, and I bet Ally might want to hang around you now because you're with a popular guy."

"I doubt it."

"Brandon still sitting by Sarah?"

"At times but they both hop around to different tables."

She pushed out the side of her cheek with her tongue. "I've got to get over him."

"Whatever happens, happens. I'll keep you posted."

At 9 p.m., Missy went home. How she missed having an everyday life, where she could hike as she pleased, spend time by the water just thinking, and alone with her journal writing her thoughts that no one had to hear but herself. She missed her freedom. She missed being Brandon's girlfriend.

Buried Secrets

***

Missy got to Nampa High, parked by Julie's Jeep, and scanned the lot to find Brandon's truck. She had ample time to socialize and enjoy lunch with Julie. Taking care of her office papers, she was glad to have a paper-free week with only online work.

As she walked to the lunchroom, she ran into friends and filled them in on what she had done with homeschool and gymnastics practice, and they congratulated her.

She was first in line to get lunch and sat at Julie's favorite table. She arrived with her lunch bag a minute later.

"Feel weird back at school?" Julie asked.

"Like I'm a stranger." She watched the students get in line.

"Looking for Brandon?"

"I miss him." She looked through the line again.

"This will help. Here comes Gabe." Julie patted the seat by her.

He sat. "Hi. You're Missy?"

"Good guess. Julie's words about me are something I might not want to know." She grinned.

"Only you are her friend, full of adventures."

"Oh, gee, thanks?" A corner of her mouth lifted.

Julie and Gabe asked her for more practice details and if she had any free time besides schoolwork. She filled them in on the hikes and how cool it was to walk on the train tracks. It helped Missy keep her mind off Brandon but her thoughts were ruined when he sat across from her. With courage, she initiated the first call. "Hi."

"What brings you to school?" Brandon asked.

"Had free time and decided I'd appear to reassure the school I was alive."

"Welcome back. Are you leaving after school?"

"I'll leave after eating the school's dry cardboard food." They laughed.

"When's your next meet?"

"The sixth at 10."

"I saw her first meet, and she's fantastic. Her hard work has paid off." Julie winked.

Missy grinned. "I try."

They talked about general stuff, the football team's last state game where they placed second. Brandon and Kaleb tried out and made the basketball team for the next semester.

She realized Brandon wasn't sitting by Kaleb or Sarah. He may have wanted to sit beside her or put on a performance. "I've heard you have a new, um, girlfriend?" She gulped.

Brandon coughed as he swallowed his food. "Oh, Sarah. Ha, ha. Her dad and my dad are working on a case together. She gets hyped and shares with me what she'd do to solve the cases better than they do."

Excellent cover. Or he doesn't like her beyond being a friend. "Sounds familiar."

Brandon labeling a person was rare. It was one clue he didn't like her beyond a friend. Missy stood. "It was fun seeing you guys, but I've got to cruise. Have a great day!"

She departed and arrived at the Murphy gym on time, returning to the reality of her obligations to practice diligently. Brandon's thoughts lingered in her mind and heart.

Chapter 24

Missy returned to practice Monday afternoon in a cheerful mood, but walking into the gym for warm-up flushed it down the toilet.

Maura needed an ego boost. "Hey, Missy Miss. Why didn't you say goodbye yesterday before you left to go home? You're becoming a Mrs. Too Good to Be Seen with Me, even in my home." Maura smirked as she smiled at Brett.

Missy sat on the floor with Echo, stretched, and cringed at the embarrassment from Maura. "It's not my job to tell you. You're not the queen of Murphy, so deal with it." She was surprised at the words that came out of her mouth with no fear. She no longer felt vulnerable and didn't care where she was placed in a friendship. Whether or not a third wheel, she refused to tolerate any more nonsense.

Maura took the sting the best she could. "I, ah, I . . . How could you say that to me?"

"What goes around comes around." Missy offered her a fake smile.

Since their group was on the floor, they moved to the side of the mat to listen to instructions.

Echo whispered, "Man, you got the nerve. Nice job. I've seen how she treats everyone. But you she hammers hard."

Missy did the splits to stretch out her legs. She longed for a new brain that wouldn't constantly gripe about her life. She had no concept of positivity and had given up on getting ahead on her schoolwork. Initially, staying ahead of the game was fun and easy, but her mind went blank after the second week of trying. She'd pushed herself too hard. Routine practice, finding buried treasures with Reed, and seeing Starr had drained her physically and emotionally. Missy hoped for a quick day and restful sleep.

Like the days before competition in the past, the remaining week was the same, but Maura's attitude got worse. Missy remained in her room, fearful of venturing outside for a walk.

***

In the darkened early Saturday morning, Maura poked her head in Missy's bedroom door. "Mom's got breakfast done."

She pulled on her anklet booties. "Almost ready." She tied the last shoe. "Nervous?"

"It's boring." She sat on the bed.

"Are you serious? These teams are better than last week."

"I only say it so I don't get nervous." Maura stood. "Let's get breakfast and go win."

Missy's instincts told her to bring home all her clothes to wash in Nampa after the meet. Maybe they needed to get rid of the air in Murphy. There wasn't much to pack because she mostly wore sweats and leotards. She loaded her car and left for the gym not too far behind Maura.

She parked by Echo and Vallie's car. As she got out, she felt pressure on her sinuses. It was probably the gymnastics meet. Two weeks in a row was demanding.

"I'm panicky as heck. You?" Echo walked in with Missy.

"I'm past any uneasiness. It causes me more problems if I do. I either do good or bad, depending on how I feel. Last week was crap. I didn't even care."

"I noticed, but we all have those moments. You feel more positive today?" Echo asked.

"I'm going to make myself feel it." Missy nodded and tried to hide her feelings so Echo wouldn't come up with a technical solution.

Warmups were over, and the competition began. First for the Owyhee gymnastics team was the bars. There were four other teams from Idaho, Oregon, and Nevada.

"Next on the bars is Melissa Mack," the announcer said. She saluted, confirmed to go, and hoped she would beat Maura on bars, but it wasn't her top priority. Missy almost missed her grip on the high bar, doing a rotation, and hoped it wasn't spotted. The other moves were great, including her landing. She got an 8.7, and Maura got a 9.2. Close, but okay.

The vault was next. Missy knew she needed to land harder on the vault board to get an inch higher on her second run, so she didn't lean on her landing. It worked, and she got a 9.6. Maura got another 9.2. A hard score to beat.

Coach Kim pulled Missy aside before her turn on the floor. "This is where you emphasize the extra moves. Remember to pretend you are showing your friends, not the judge. I want to see you move like a fish."

"It will be done." She saluted and got positioned on the floor. The routine went smoothly, but the judges deducted two points for the intentional fall, despite it being part of the routine. She got a 9.8, and Maura got a 9.7. *Even a tiny lead is better than none.*

Reed had finished his responsibilities in the gym and sat by Missy and Julie on the bench. The last rotation on the beam began. Maura finished her routine and sat on the bench behind her.

Julie turned around. "Good job, Maura, on stopping your fall. I'm saying it as truth, not to be mean."

"Thanks." She went poker-faced.

"Your turn, Missy." Coach Kim nodded. Reed rubbed her back as she got up. She stretched her arms, bent over to stretch her back, and mounted the beam.

Missy's Chinese split mount was perfect, along with her moves. On dismounting, she added a twist to her double backflip and, again, landed perfectly.

She put on her sweats and sat with Reed and Julie. Reed rested his hand on her lower back. "Your hard work paid off."

Julie clapped her hands. "Oh, my gosh. You were perfect." All she could do was smile.

The four judges marked the score and announced, "10, 10, 10, and 10."

Echo sprung to her feet, dragged Missy off the bench, and hugged her. Reed grabbed her arm, pulled her out of Echo's arms, and gave her a quick kiss and a bear hug.

A movement caught Missy's eye, and she peered out the window at the foyer. She saw Brandon standing with hands in his pockets. Reed praised her, but she didn't hear a word. Her face went numb. She pushed Reed away with her hands. Brandon turned and walked out the door.

She wanted to run after him, but Maura, who'd seen it all, stopped her.

"Running after him won't make a difference. He saw the kiss and hug. You're history with Brandon." Maura's face lit up, but Missy's heart sank. They weren't officially boyfriend and girlfriend, but there was something there. She'd felt it at the lunchroom table. She'd felt it as he'd spoken to her. And now she'd lost him for good.

Brandon.

"What's wrong? Are you embarrassed to be seen with me in public?" Reed asked. "Is there something I should know?"

"I don't feel good." Missy pulled away.

Reed followed. "You need to stay to get your trophy. I know you got no lower than second place." He rubbed both hands on her arms.

She was lost. The person she loved most saw Reed kiss her.

"Please don't. It hurts my arms. My body's sick, and I must go." The announcer called all gymnasts to form a line on the floor. She walked to the area and stood by Echo and Staci.

"Good luck to you both. You all did a superb job." Missy halfheartedly smiled, looking back to the foyer where she had last seen him.

"Missy, you did the best," Echo cheered her on. "I can't believe your beam routine. You looked like a pro."

Tears welled up in Missy's eyes as the winners were announced, but her emotions differed from those around her.

"Tony for Men's All-Around!"

"Maura, first on bars and second on vault!"

"Echo, first on vault and third on floor!"

Missy stood silently as her scores were read, still thinking of Brandon and the ache in her soul.

"Missy, first on beam and floor!" There was a huge cheer. On the overall scores, she'd received first place. Echo came in second, just half a point ahead of Maura in third.

The teammates gave hugs, congratulations, and extra yahoos to Missy. Maura gave her a high five. Reed got busy cleaning the gym, so it was easy for Missy to avoid him.

A few minutes later, she waved goodbye to Echo and exchanged ciao-for-now with her other teammates. She breathed a sigh of relief at the outer door, and, by habit, drove to the Derringers' instead of Nampa. She threw the rest of her items in a box and thanked Mrs. Derringer for her hospitality.

"I'm taking a long vacation," she said. "I need time alone. Again, thanks for having me be your guest."

"You are family and always welcome here," Mrs. Derringer replied. She smiled slightly, looking into Missy's eyes. "Be good."

Missy shoved the trophies and box in the back seat and left for home. Her home. She intended to stay there for a long time.

Chapter 25

Jamming to the Top 40s, Missy cruised home feeling on top of the world. Her decision to quit was the right one. She'd felt trapped in a life she didn't like. While it was good to stand out, flushing her personal life down the toilet made little sense.

Reed was a rebound, and she knew he didn't like her—not really. She was his show and tell. It was for show, to tell people she was his prize gymnast. Or perhaps he thought she'd understand about Starr and the hidden treasures.

She was done with fame and glory, although it had been fun while it lasted. She had an inkling for Reed, but knew it wasn't love. The look in Brandon's eyes when she saw him said everything. She wanted her everyday life back with friends, fights with her little brother, and pushing her parents' limits.

As she pulled into the driveway, Missy didn't see her parents' car and she remembered they were at an all-day business party.

She unpacked and let her hair down, observing a transformed reflection in the mirror. Perhaps she needed to experience a different part of the world to mature. She twisted her hair and thought of Maura.

She checked her wallet. Yes, she had enough for a haircut. Smiling, she slid back into her car and drove to Razzle Dazzle Hair Salon. No more hair care pain in the butt, including buns.

Missy propped her arms on the hair salon clerk's desk and smiled. "Please, please let there be an opening." she pleaded. "Is Debbie in?"

Peggy tapped the pen on the appointment calendar. "Lucky for you, there was a cancellation. We'll be ready for you in ten minutes."

"Happy times."

"We got new hairstyle books in. They are on the coffee table." Peggy pointed.

She sat, flipped through a few books, unsure of the ideal hairstyle for long hair. Her bangs hung long enough to put behind her ears. Missy had to clip them during practice and competition to keep them off her face. Even though she won first place, she wouldn't be surprised if people still labeled her the All-around Klutz. Two books later, she still didn't see a hairstyle she liked.

Debbie came to the waiting room followed by an elderly lady with silver hair. "Enjoy your day, Helen," and noticed her new appointment. "Melissa?"

She followed Debbie back to her booth. "Your hair." She took a handful and ran her hand through it. "It's the longest I've seen it."

Missy sat in the chair as Debbie wrapped the apron around her neck. "My head feels heavy." They laughed.

"An inch or two trim?"

Her stomach twitched again. "I want a new creative look, and I trust you."

"You sure? Length doesn't matter?"

"Nope."

Debbie led the way to the hair-wash booth. The warm water hit Missy's head. She loved getting her hair washed or massaged the way Debbie did it.

"How's Brandon?"

Keeping her eyes closed, she pretended not to hear the question.

Back at Deb's booth, she brushed Missy's hair. "You're positive I can have fun with your hair?"

"I trust you. You can manipulate my hair the best." She closed her eyes, not wanting to see the new creation. "Have fun."

"Oh, I will."

The scissors clipped, clipped, and clipped. Missy's head felt lighter and lighter as the hair landed on the floor.

"Okay, sleepyhead. I think you'll like the style. It enhances your teen-like image while projecting a confident aura." She undid the apron.

Her eyes widened in astonishment as she gazed at her incredible haircut. The look portrayed her as vigorous and sophisticated. The bangs were long enough to be tucked behind her ears, while the rest reached her shoulders with a subtle layered style, adding volume. She loved it.

"Oh, Debbie, it's awesome. Thank you so much."

"Your eyes say it all. Now, go out and show the world."

The next stop was to get a peanut parfait at Dairy King. *Watch out, world. Melissa Mack's on her way.* Instead of going inside to sit, she opted to get two through the drive-in window. Julie deserved a treat.

Rachel Brown, Julie's mom, answered the door. It took her a second to realize who was standing there. She gave lots of niceties about Missy's haircut. "Julie will be happy to see you." She let her in. "She's in her room and will like her treat."

Missy tiptoed down the stairs and knocked on Julie's door.

"Come in, Mom."

She turned the knob on Julie's door and stuck her hand holding the parfait through a partial opening.

Julie shrieked, "Missy, get in here!" She grabbed the treat and pushed the door open. "Oh, my heck. Look at you. When did you cut your hair?"

"Fifteen minutes ago. Do you like it?"

"I love it. Want to go for a motorcycle ride?" Julie rarely asked such questions. Missy frequently asked and even led them on an unsafe trail. Julie had flown over a small hill and gotten a flat tire. She believed Julie still blamed her for it.

"Nah, can't mess up my new hairdo." She tossed her head around.

"Or you don't wish to see Brandon."

Her lips quivered. She tried to control her emotions.

"Don't you like the haircut? Or you'd rather not see Brandon?"

"I left the team."

Julie looked confused. "You left?"

She bowed her head and cried.

"Missy, what's wrong?" Julie searched the side of her bed for the tissue box and hugged her. She recounted to Julie every place she had been in Murphy, from start to finish, mentioning Reed, Tony, Echo, and Maura. She added the hiking, looking for Starr, and that Reed was a good kisser. Her words lacked emotion, only facts, though her tears were a floodgate.

"What made it worse is Brandon saw Reed kissing me after my score. I saw the hurt in his face."

"I don't know what to do, but I'm here to listen to your confusing life. Hold on a minute." She came back with two large glasses of root beer and ice. "Drink this. It will get you hydrated again. You lost a lot of water with your tears."

Missy laughed. Julie had a knack for injecting humor into her life. "Thanks. I do have a messed-up life."

"You got your stuff and left?"

She swallowed her soda pop. "Yep. One of my spur-of-the-moment deals."

Julie opened her mouth in aye. "You are a brave soul. I wonder what Maura will think when she noticed you went AWALL."

"It hasn't hit me yet and to tell you the truth. I don't care. I'm done being a worry wart."

"Good choice. You were about to pop. Speaking of good things, Brandon has not been sitting with Sarah. I guess he still likes you if he came to see you at your meet."

A tear came back. "Julie, he looked so hurt. All the color and happiness drained from his face. I'm scared."

After two hours of talking, Missy went home and greeted her family, who arrived shortly after. They adored her haircut. She showed her trophies, ribbons, and pictures. Her dad hugged her.

"Hey, Missy. Can I take your ribbons and trophies to school on Monday to show my friends?" Tommy beamed.

"How about bringing your friends here next Saturday to show them?"

"I guess it's okay."

She motioned for her mom to follow her to her room.

"What's wrong? I know leaving a dream you had is hard." Her mom sat by Missy on the bed.

"I understand the feeling of hard work," Missy began. "Reaching the top only fuels the desire to work even harder. I guess I got tired of my 'on top of the world' feeling. I want my normal, boring life back."

"So, you're not continuing?"

Missy shook her head.

"I get it. The good news is now you know. Anything else?"

"Mom, can I ask you a question?"

"Of course, you can. I'll bet you a Dairy King peanut parfait I'll understand." She handed her a pillow and kept one for herself. They sat back on the bed and hugged the pillows. Missy remembered the pillow hugging with her mom years ago.

"Is it possible to have feelings for two different people simultaneously?" she asked.

"Meaning you like two different boys? I haven't heard of a new person or a name besides Brandon."

"Reed is Coach Pat's son. He helped at the gym when he had time. He had other jobs to do, too. At first contact, we knew we liked each other." Missy glanced out her window at the empty field. "He invited me to go hiking with him. Oh, I forgot to tell you, on our first night at the Bells' house, Coach Pat told us to stay off the train track because it was hard to hear the train until it was too late."

"Are you going to admit being on the forbidden track?" Her mom shook her head.

"Yes, but I was with Reed. I'm unsure how to express it, even though I'm being scattered."

"Go ahead, because I'm not leaving until I hear it all."

"Pat has seen Starr. And to top it off, his wife Chaundra is his fourth or fifth granddaughter."

Mom exhaled loudly. "You were out late at night with Reed looking for Chief Starr's ghost?"

"Yes. But it wasn't late at night, and we weren't gone long." Missy bit her lower lip. "I saw him, Mom. His ghostly figure rode along the side of Amtrak. He looked at us, nodded, and rode on."

"You saw a spirit?"

"Yes. I know it sounds weird, but I believe it."

Her mom nodded. "Reed is the other boy you like?"

Crap, I can't tell my mom about the cave or that I heard rocks thrown by a possible ghost. "Mom, what was Jim like when you first started dating? Was he nice, or did he only want to play kissy-face with you?"

"Kissy-face? Interesting phrase." She took Missy's hand and placed her other one on top. "Jim was a free-spirited kind of guy everyone liked. I still can't understand why he liked me, but he could see that I was always genuine. Do you think Brandon is using you, and Reed is the better choice, even if he doesn't live close?"

Now for the hard part. Missy had to tell her. "Maybe I'm scared because I don't know how to deal with it. Okay, I know I'm almost sixteen. Is it natural to like a guy? You did."

"It's natural, but be careful you don't get hurt. Try to keep a causal relationship. You still have many years before you need to get serious."

Missy's mom made her feel comfortable at times and appreciated that her mom seemed to understand a little when it came to boys.

"I told Reed a little about my nightmares and seeing Starr's chief once or twice in the field." Her mom clearly admired her imagination but refrained from saying so. Missy continued. "He told me he knew I understood why he was looking for Starr. There's a lot more, but it isn't important. Brandon was there, that's what I mean. He's the main reason I left. Brandon saw the show. After getting my tens on the beam, Reed picked me up in a hug, spun me around, and kissed me. I saw Brandon, and the look on his face killed me."

Tears welled in Missy's eyes. She couldn't finish.

Her mom wrapped her arms around her and held her tight. "Oh, sweetie, you're torn between two boys liking you."

"It's a different feeling with Reed. I can't explain it. Brandon crossed my mind. I couldn't get rid of him."

She tucked Missy's loose hair behind her ear. "Can I tell you a secret?"

"Yes."

"I still have a soft spot in my heart for Jim. Despite his current state as a bad person, I choose to remember the goodness he was.

Missy leaned on her mom's shoulder. "Thank you. I'd rather be single if I can't have Brandon."

"You need to tell your coach you won't be returning."

"I get it. I'll do it tomorrow."

Later in the evening as Missy got ready for bed, she felt an anxiety attack building and thought it best to take some acetaminophen PM tablets. Sad to say, it didn't help her mind.

Sleep led to nightmares.

Missy arrived at the Bells' house and met with Pat and Reed in the barn.

"I'm here to tell you I'm done with gymnastics and on the team. I'm done being used as bait to find Starr and drug hideouts," she began.

Jim appeared around a haystack and laughed at Reed. "I should have told you about Missy. She will drag your heart down and flush it." He stepped right up to Reed's face. Missy expected Pat to intervene, but he mysteriously disappeared.

"As if you know her. I know what I'm dealing with. You are the one using me to chase down people to buy your Twist and find places to make it." Reed stepped back and held up his fist.

"Ay, the teen way to deal with stress. Fight. You are a waste of my time. I can get more to help me. I trusted you, so why did you get Missy involved?"

The bickering continued for another minute, escalating Missy's fear of a fistfight. It almost happened until Starr appeared between Reed and Jim. Looking at Missy, he pushed both men away and declared, "You are needed."

She sat up in bed. *Needed for what?*

Chapter 26

Missy became nervous as the view of Murphy got closer. Facing Coach Pat and talking to Reed terrified her, especially after her unsettling dream, but she had no choice. She couldn't leave him clueless.

Missy got to the Bells' house and was relieved when Chaundra opened the door.

"Hi. Reed told me you were sick. Are you feeling better?" Chaundra let her in. "I like your haircut."

"Thanks, and yes, I'm doing better. Is Coach Pat here?" Missy rubbed her hands on her thighs.

"Pat and Reed are both in the barn. Take the back door downstairs for a shorter route."

"Thank you." Missy went on her way. She didn't know what to expect. Would Reed understand? Would he sulk or get mad at her?

With a rake, Pat walked out of the barn door. He saw Missy and smiled. "Reed's in the barn with the hay." He kept walking.

"Coach Pat." He stopped. "Um, I came back to tell you I'm officially withdrawing from your team. It's nothing personal with you, Kirk, the other coaches, or any team members. It's my choice. I'm sorry, but thank you for training and allowing me to join your team." She rubbed her legs again.

He didn't show any signs of anger, but did seem sad. "I appreciate your honesty, and we will miss you. Remember, a place awaits if you come back." He shook her hand and pointed to the barn door where Reed was.

The conversation with Pat was unexpectedly easy, but she was unsure about Reed. In the barn, Missy spotted Reed filling a bucket with oats for the horses. She didn't know if she should run into his arms or stand there like she didn't want to touch him.

A part of her liked Reed, but an even greater part of her loved Brandon. "Hi."

Surprised, Reed dropped the bucket, stepped closer, and stopped, running his hand through her hair. "I like your haircut, but I like you better." He kissed her.

Missy let him and told herself it was a goodbye kiss. The kiss got longer, past her comfort, and she pushed him off.

"Scared Dad will walk in and catch us? He knows we're a couple." He put his arm around her. Missy stepped around so she could look at him.

"Reed, I like you, but it won't work. I got my stuff from the Derringers and moved back home. I'm done living a life I don't want."

"What?"

She scratched her nose. "Long-distance relationships don't work. At least not for us. You're free. Please don't feel you have to stay with me."

Reed shifted his look from her to the barn door after a few seconds. "You know, it wasn't a serious relationship, anyway. All I wanted was to kiss you."

She felt a self-slap in the face and glanced around the barn with its mixed smell of animals and hay. "Honestly, I used you back to take my mind off another person." She shrugged. "I guess we're even. I didn't want to leave without telling you, so I did my deed. Bye, Reed. It was fun while it lasted."

Exiting the barn, Missy turned around when she felt Reed's touch on her arm and looked up at him. He was grinning. Did he understand?

"I think we were both having fun," he said. "Friends?"

Missy didn't know when she would be back, but having Reed as a friend was the logical choice. "Sure," she offered and extended her hand. "Friends."

He took it and gave a light squeeze. Maybe he loved her. After she was gone, she imagined he stood outside the barn where she'd left him and watched her leave.

When Missy got home, she sat on the couch to watch TV and relax. No pressure to practice on a routine, or deal with Maura's manipulations. Not being able to see Reed again flushed out of her mind with no more hiking in the mountains to find hidden treasures or nightmares. *Old wives' tale, I bet.* She was home sweet home.

The doorbell rang. "Missy, Julie's here," Tommy said.

She made herself at home and sat on the couch by Missy.

"Bored?"

"More like I can't believe I'm home for good." She adjusted herself to face Julie better. "How's Gabe?"

"I would have been at the ranch with him today, but I had this strong feeling I should spend time with you before you embark on another adventure in a new town."

"Ha. Not going to happen."

Julie leaned forward, sternly. "I'll believe it when I see it." She grabbed Missy's hand. "Come on. I'm taking you for a drive."

Missy hesitated as fear crossed over.

"If you see Brandon, you see Brandon."

"Okay. No more delays, it's time to confront the world." After she grabbed her wallet, she told her mom she was off with Julie. She ran outside and jumped into Julie's Jeep.

"Hit Dairy King first?" Julie asked.

"Before facing the world, let's check Horizon for a sale."

"You are brave."

"Cross my fingers five times so I'm not doomed with a failure to socialize."

"Oh, stop the blubber."

"You forgot one place after Horizon."

"What?" Julie found a parking spot at the mall.

"Foosball."

"Now you're talking."

Missy and Julie hit Horizon first and tried on the new jeans they had displayed. She came out of the dressing room. Julie shook her head. Missy glanced at her reflection in the mirror and felt like puking. It looked like a sack was hanging off her bottom.

The salesclerk cantered over to see. "Oh, those jeans look perfect. Should I fetch a black pair for you to try on next?" She put on a fake smile.

"You're kidding me, right?" Julie pulled a face. She'd changed, too, in the past year. Bolder and not as shy with strangers.

"Of course not." The clerk was speechless and left them to help another customer.

Missy changed back into her jeans, and they hightailed it out of the store.

Julie laughed. "I can't believe I said it."

"You took me by surprise, too. Did you notice the salesclerk's expression? I thought she was going to faint.

Priceless." They checked out a couple of other clothing stores before a new idea hit Missy.

"Red Baron Arcade, here we come." Missy took the last bite of the cookie they purchased at Little Chipmunk. "You ready to get hammered by the foosball pro?"

"Ha, mind you, I'm not bad myself. I have an eye for the offense. Your perfection is the goal." Julie made a fist.

"My defense isn't bad."

"True."

Julie checked for an open table while Missy got coins from the money machine. She turned to see Julie waving. Two people were standing next to her. It couldn't be. But it was. As she neared, Brandon and Kaleb turned to grin at her. She tried to grin. Not good. Her palms sweated. "Hey."

They smiled as Julie got excited. "We got ourselves a dual match." She walked to the other side of the table, and Missy followed. "Since this is the only table left."

"You'll kill us in a minute," Missy smirked. Her only hope was they weren't pros and would not slaughter them.

Brandon looked at Missy as he held the ball to make the first drop. "How was the competition on Saturday?"

Crap. How could can I pull this off? Act natural, act natural. Breathe deep. "Okay. With a competition the week prior and another one scheduled for this Saturday, it required more effort." *Do I tell him I'm a quitter and not going back? Kaleb would agree I was a quitter.*

Julie butted in. "Don't be shy." She pointed at Missy and looked at Brandon and Kaleb. "You need to congratulate this talented young lady on getting all tens on the beam. Plus, she got first place overall."

Kaleb nodded, and Brandon's face flashed a mixture of emotions before a smile. "Congratulations. I bet your team's happy."

"Thank you."

"Let's get the game on." Brandon dropped the ball.

Missy got the ball, moved it to the middle, lifted the back of her plastic players, and smacked it hard into the goal.

Kaleb threw back his arms.

Missy took the ball out of the goal, glanced at Brandon, and watched him smile. It wasn't his usual friendly smile. It scared her.

"Put the ball in the slot, Mack. One point isn't the winning number," Kaleb sneered.

She gave Julie a warning glance, signaling her to step back and let the guys score a couple of goals. The competition was on. Missy dropped the ball and made a stupid move as Julie blocked one goal, but let one go in. Kaleb's head appeared to grow bigger and Missy prayed it would pop. He drove her crazy.

The score was eight to five in Brandon's favor. Missy and Julie were ready to make a comeback. Kaleb put in the ball. Missy moved the ball to the side and positioned the plastic players for a perfectly angled shot.

They scored five goals quickly and watched Kaleb's head shrink with each point. *It feels good even if my head's a little bigger.* Missy grinned.

Brandon, gracious in defeat, sprinkled compliments during the game: "Excellent shot." "Nice Move." and "What a block!" Kaleb, perhaps a tad salty, attributed it to "beginner's luck," while Missy responded with an eye roll.

As the four headed to I Scream You Scream, Brandon confidently led the way. The promise of a treat for the losers hung in the air. Kaleb stepped up, placed his order, and paid. The sweet taste of victory or defeat awaited them in icy delights.

"The usual?" Brandon elbowed Missy.

"Yes, please."

"Peanut parfait with extra nuts, banana split, and?" He looked at Julie.

"Strawberry shortcake."

Brandon paid. They got their treats and sat in a booth. The girls sat side by side with Missy on the edge facing Brandon.

They talked about the game and how the girls slaughtered them. It seemed Kaleb half-listened. He wasn't happy he lost. Julie was the chattiest, with Brandon offering only a few comments. Missy occasionally contributed a word or two.

In between bites, Kaleb perked. "Have any nightmares of Jim digging a grave for you lately?" Brandon didn't say a word, and Julie looked at Missy in horror.

Missy pushed her parfait aside. "Grow up, Kaleb." She was going to pop any minute. She stood up, headed to the main corridor of the building, and walked.

"Missy, wait," Brandon called.

"Why?" She stopped and eyed him with a glare of death.

"Don't let Kaleb get to you."

"You think that's the only problem?"

"Are you okay?"

"You don't seem to care. I'm uncertain if there was ever anything between us." Missy took a step closer to look up into his Brandon's eyes. "I'm sorry, but this has been building up, and I haven't known how to deal with it or how to approach you.

Brandon put his hands in his front pockets.

"One reason I moved in with Maura was to know my true feelings. Was I vulnerable? Heck, yeah. I know you were there on Saturday. I saw you when Reed kissed me. But do you blame me for falling for a guy who gave me attention? If so, it's your fault."

Brandon returned her stare.

She leaned closer. "Do I still like you? Yes, excessively. It scares me to death. But I shouldn't give you the attitude without an explanation."

People walked by, stared, and snickered. Julie tapped her back. "Missy, you're drawing attention, and it's time to go home." She pulled her away from Brandon. He stood still, like a statue.

She gave him one last look.

And then the words came. She wasn't sure if she'd heard them correctly or if he'd even spoken them at all.

"I love you." He whispered the words.

She was sure he didn't mean for her to hear them. *Perhaps those are the words I wished he'd say?* Missy opened her mouth, but nothing came out. Julie gave one last pull on her arm, and they took off. She was silent as they left the mall.

Julie didn't ask until they left the parking lot. "Man, you let him have it. What did you say? I'm a little shocked because you never lose control of your emotions. What did Brandon say?" She reached the end of the lot and merged onto the main road.

"He said he loved me."

She slammed on the brakes halfway out into the road. "What?" A car honked behind them. She got on the road and glanced at Missy.

"It sure sounded like it. What else rhymes with love? I glove you. I dove you. I like you. I adore you." Nothing nice or mean sounded like love. *How could he love me? We aren't even a couple.*

The trip to Missy's house was spent in silence. Julie dropped her off and advised her to call for a chat later. She wasn't sure what to say. Would her life be smoother moving back home? *Who am I kidding? I am a scared little kitty cat who can't face reality.* Perhaps she needed to erase Brandon from her life for good and deal with it. *Perhaps?*

Chapter 27

Missy had Julie take her to school on Monday. She figured if she drove, she'd, without a doubt, leave early if her emotions took control.

"Not sleep well?" Julie backed out onto the road from the Macks' driveway.

"It shows?"

"A little. Your nervousness about going back to school is clear, and everyone will be curious about why you left the gymnastics team. Music filled the air, ending communication until she pulled into the school and parked on the passenger side of Brandon's truck.

"Why'd you park here?" Missy pulled a face.

"My goodness, it's not like the truck will put itself in gear and run over us. You sound like you hate Brandon after yesterday."

Missy got out and cringed. "I want to pretend I can't stand him and have a day without emotions. And I don't want to remember what I heard him say. I'm confused." She shut the Jeep's door harder than needed. Julie gave a warning look. "Sorry."

Julie raised her hands. "See you at lunch?"

They walked through the parking lot to the school.

"Yep. I get to go to the office and get re-situated with my attendance." She watched Julie enter Building 1, where Brandon currently had a class.

Sitting in classes and listening to a teacher give instructions wasn't Missy's thing. She missed doing schoolwork on her own and with an aide if needed. But she didn't miss the cramped room in Murphy. In between the two classes, she walked by Ally who gave her a look of, 'My life was fine without seeing you.'

Julie sat at their table in the lunchroom, eating her salad, when Missy arrived with her spaghetti. "Spaghetti is sickening with or without sauce." Julie pulled a disgusted face.

"I love eating worms." Missy sucked one noodle slowly, with the sauce dripping off. "Did you see Brandon?"

"I was waiting for you to ask before saying anything. He entered, grabbed lunch, and left. I didn't see Kaleb or his other friends. Maybe they brought lunch and are meeting outside." She crunched on a carrot.

"Is he hiding out with Sarah?"

Julie scanned the lunchroom, poked Missy's arm, and pointed to the right. "Three tables over. She's there with other friends."

She wanted to leave without witnessing Brandon returning the lunch tray. "Can I use your keys? My favorite pen fell out of my backpack."

Julie dug her keys out of her backpack. "Here."

"I'll meet you after school." She took care of her tray and walked to the Jeep. If she'd had her car, she would have left. She opened the Jeep's door, sat on the passenger's side and gazed out the window feeling a stare. She turned. Brandon was sitting in his truck, eyes on her. Not what she needed.

Missy covered her face with her hands. She tried to hate Brandon and all males alive, minus her dad and Tommy. Three taps sounded on the window. She opened the door for Brandon.

She looked at his face and wished she hadn't. Tears ran down her cheeks. Brandon pulled so her head rested on his shoulder, and he moved the bangs off her forehead.

"Don't cry. You should hate me." He wiped the tears off her cheeks.

"I tried to hate you today but can't make myself. Tried liking Reed, but it didn't work either in my attempt to escape. My thoughts of you persisted, preventing me from getting far." She cried again.

"I'm the one to blame. I'm scared. My dad has moved us many times. I don't want to get caught up in my new life, school, and friends only to leave again." He touched Missy's face with both hands. "Last year, I asked my mom if we were moving again after our first meeting. She reassured me we weren't, but things change."

The school bell rang for the next class. They ignored it. "I saw you Saturday," Missy admitted. "Maura stopped me from running after you; said you were history."

"It doesn't matter. I am present, and you are too." He kissed her forehead.

"Did you say what I thought you said Saturday at the mall?" She looked at Brandon, embarrassed, and hoped she wasn't wrong.

His face turned red. She'd never seen him embarrassed. "True emotions are stronger than wanting not to say it. I'm scared of feeling this way, but I love you."

Her mouth quivered. She placed her hands on Brandon's. "I . . . I . . . love you, too. I can't get you out of my mind." He leaned over and kissed her.

It was a long kiss, and she didn't pull back. When the kiss broke, she looked into his eyes. "I think I need to get to class," she murmured.

"P.E. for me, and I don't care." He stood. "Want me to give you a ride home today?"

She exited the Jeep and locked it. "I have Julie's keys, so I'll go with her." Her emotions were numb, making it impossible for her to express her feelings to Brandon, at least for the time being. Lost in the realm of love, she felt as if her feet didn't touch the ground, even after stepping out of the car.

Brandon smiled and headed back to class. He turned once and waved at her.

***

After school, Missy met Julie on the sidewalk, walked to her Jeep, and jingled her keys. "It's official."

Julie grabbed the keys from her. "You're dropping out of school for good and joining the circus. You'll be doing your gymnastics moves on the tightrope. I knew it. You're running away from me, Brandon, and life."

Missy play-fisted her best friend's arm. "Oh, stop it. I'm in love. Not puppy love. And I'm being loved back. *Eek.*"

"It's about time it's official."

"I should ask you about Gabe. You two seem tight as a knot."

"I had to replace you, remember?"

"Nice. Was it love at first sight for both of us? Are we too young to commit? Are we too young to fall in love? Is it actual love or puppy love?"

"Slow down there, Miss Motor Mouth."

"I try," Missy said with exhaustion.

"Not hard enough," Julie scolded.

"But will it mess up our lives hanging out like normal?"

"Being friends with you isn't normal. I'll take what I can get."

"Seriously?"

"We're fine. I'm a 'sit back and watch life pass by' person unless I'm on my horse. You bring out parts of me I'd never think of doing. But I'm glad I don't have a boring life anymore being your friend."

"I suppose I can take that as a compliment." It made Missy remember how crazy last year was; meeting Brandon, seeing an actual ghost, and encountering her mom's high school boyfriend, Jim, who was back in town causing trouble.

Julie pulled into Missy's driveway. "Please leave so I can do my homework. Love you."

"Love you, too."

Chapter 28

Jim and Dwight dropped off their last box of Twist to a customer in Mountain Home. "Glad the roads are dry. In the olden days, we've had white Thanksgivings and Christmases. The mountains look bare, too." Jim turned the ignition. "Time for food. Freeway or Murphy route?"

"Not Thanksgiving yet," Dwight rubbed his stomach, "but the thought of chewing on a turkey leg makes me realize I'm starving."

Jim ignored Dwight's comment. "Pretty pleasant not owing money to Rock or Carlos. We are on our own."

"Should we try the recipe your grandma gave you? Raise the ante if it's better?"

"During the holiday season, we can provide a discounted trial price. If they're satisfied, they can opt for a higher payment. Time to eat a meal at your daughter's first."

They drove in silence, occupied by the radio playing music. Jim parked in the alley, and they snuck in the back door at Jenkins' Antique Store.

"Ruth. Your hungry dad's here," Dwight called, not knowing if the store was open or closed.

They heard Ruth stomp down the stairs. "You're alive. Don't answer your calls; your messages are full, so I can't leave one." Though she sounded upset, she hugged her dad. "Where have you been?"

"Traveling, selling, and living. We're set to build our merchandise and have repeating customers for our products."

Jim tried to cover their product even though he knew Ruth knew it all. "Our storage units are a hit. The most popular size is the smallest." He looked around for signs of food.

"If you answered your phone and didn't avoid my calls, you would've known the cops have visited me several times asking me questions about you two," Ruth said.

Jim worked hard to keep his expression neutral and handed Ruth an envelope. "Help with your bills."

She took it and counted the money. "Five hundred dollars. Money must be fine." She looked at her dad.

Dwight raised his eyebrows.

"I know you prefer to keep a low profile during the day." Ruth placed the money in a jar on the counter.

"We hoped there was food easy to grab and eat." Dwight guided himself to the fridge and opened it.

"Sorry to disappoint you. I have frozen TV dinners. No leftovers." Following a brief chat, Jim and Dwight departed to visit a drive-through.

Chapter 29

Missy took a paper out and jotted ideas for her and Julie in their speech class presentation. They needed visual instructions on any subject. She imagined herself as a gymnastics instructor, with Julie showing splits and somersaults to the class. It would be funny, but she knew Julie would decline. Food sounded better and she had the best recipe for a cheesecake.

Ally was also in the speech class and had only said 'Hi' once since she returned to school and treated her like a stranger. She never said a word to Julie, either. She felt bad. Maura was Ally's heart and blood pumping through her veins to keep her alive.

The phone rang, but she didn't answer the one in her room. "Missy, phone call," Tommy yelled.

She rolled her eyes, wanting to maintain her train of thought without interruptions. "Hey there, to whoever's calling."

"Hi. It's Echo. How are you?"

"I'm here. You? I miss talking to you." The last words came uncomfortably from her lips.

"Me too. Sorry for the short notice, but we have a harvest dinner dance on Saturday night. Same place as the

Halloween one. There's still the corn maze, too. Can you come?"

"I'll see if my boyfriend wants to go. Time?"

"Five. I can't wait to see you."

She'd only go if Brandon would, so she called him. "Want to hit the boonies this Saturday for dinner and dance? I'll drive."

"Sounds fun," Brandon said.

Julie was next on the list to call. She went over her idea about the cheesecake, and Julie agreed. They hit the store after school the next day and spent the evening at Julie's house baking.

"Too bad there isn't an oven to cook it in class. We'll have to throw the batter away." Julie stirred the brown sugar into the melted cream cheese.

"If we had a stove, we could do our famous caramel corn," Missy suggested.

"A sticky mess for sure."

"I agree one hundred percent. We can bring home the demo. Cross your fingers that it won't spill on the drive home. Then we can cook it. But it's a pain to carry it around and not spill everywhere."

Julie laughed. "You could accidentally spill it on Ally."

"A mean trick, but I like it." Missy touched Julie's arm. "Ask Gabe if he wants to join us for a holiday dinner and dance in Murphy this Saturday. Brandon's coming with me."

"Gabe's got a horse show, and I'm going to help him."

"Sounds fun."

"It is." She squeezed her shoulders in tight and smiled.

Missy watched a family ride by on their bikes on the road out the kitchen window as the cheesecake baked. "You know, it doesn't seem like I've been gone for months."

"It seems like forever since you first left." The timer buzzed.

Julie put the cake in the oven. They'd used a casserole dish to triple the recipe. "Smells delicious."

"It'll be better after it's cooked." She helped Julie pack their items for class the next day and went home.

***

Speech class had some hilarious topics. One student showed how to make an animal out of a balloon. One demonstration was how to create a perfect paper airplane. Boring.

Next in line was Missy and Julie, who put on chef hats and lifted a wooden spoon. "Come one, come all. With my helper," she extended her arm toward Missy, who stood beside her, "you will learn how to make the best cheesecake in Nampa, Idaho."

Missy handed Julie the pre-measured ingredients for her to put in the bowl. "Next are the eggs." When attempting to crack it, gravity caused the egg to slip from her hand and fall to the floor.

The class, including Missy and Julie, laughed until Ally yelled, "Always a klutz." Missy looked at Julie and winked. It was payback time.

"After baking the cake, let it cool at room temperature for twenty to thirty minutes before putting on the topping." Julie pointed at the sample dish. "There are plenty of flavors to use. Here you have a choice of blueberry or cherry."

Students who wanted one received small squares of cheesecake. Missy offered Ally a sample and made herself "accidentally" trip. Since she had a small piece on her plate, the mess was minimal. The pie fell on Ally's thigh.

"I guess you're right. I am a klutz." Ally's face was astonished, and the laugh was back on her. Everyone laughed again, including the teacher.

Missy wasn't used to being a snot. She caught herself biting her cuticles, and after class, she made it a point to pull Ally aside.

"It wasn't nice what I did, and I'm sorry. Returning the negativity, you gave me felt satisfying, at least initially."

"You've changed, and I accept your apology," Ally folded her arms. "I've learned I can't always get what I want." She smiled and left.

Julie leaned against the wall. She had heard what had transpired between them. "Did Ally mean it?" she asked.

"I have no idea, but it sounded nice," Missy said. "With Maura gone, maybe Ally has changed, too."

Friday night, Ally called and invited Missy over. She went. They ate blackberry cheesecake. Perhaps her cake-dropping had made a point.

Chapter 30

"It's sure dark in here." Dwight eased his way down the ladder at Red Line Autos into the tunnel behind Jim and his flashlight.

"Still scared of the dark? Turn on the generator." Jim suggested.

"Stop reminding me of the tunnel ghosts."

"You're the one who told me about the ghosts and floating spirits. We've been in caves and tunnels for weeks. Why the change?"

"Tired of being a hermit, mole, living under the ground," Dwight complained.

"Soon, Dwight, soon. We'll leave Nampa and return to Arizona, or perhaps somewhere new. I hear Tri-Cities in Washington is an excellent area."

Dwight opened a can of beer. "How much do the Murphy people need?"

"Ten pints. Five thousand dollars in our hands."

"The sound of money is a natural high." He exuded confidence and authority as he inspected the machines, striding around with his head held high. "Who are we selling to today in Nampa?"

"No one today, just making a stock. Let's hurry to Murphy and start the machines. David and Leo will make a purchase." Jim spit on his fingers and ran it through his hair. "Guess we need to get going."

As part of their routine, they grabbed breakfast at a drive-in on the way to the cave in Murphy. Jim continued to talk about the money coming soon and what they could do with it. They could spend it on anything they wanted, travel the world. Life looked good.

They had gotten a great deal on another generator to keep the electricity on for hours before recharging. A batch of Twist on the new burner was quicker, and the bonus was more locals joining to distribute Twist in the surrounding area. Yes, Jim was happy.

Dwight snorted a second round of Twist. "Aren't you worried you'll run into Nancy Drew and one of the Hardy Boys?"

"Don't worry. We'll get a mother lode of Twist made and hightail it out of Murphy Cave Land, Idaho for good."

As the drug machines ran, both men vegged out in their sleeping area and tried to relax. Jim heard voices and sat up. "Visitors?"

"Aren't you the one who told me David and Leo were coming?"

As if deaf and not wanting to hear his mess-ups, Jim stood and met his customers in the main room. "Sorry, we ran late and the product won't be ready for a couple more hours." He shrugged.

"Okay, man," David said. "Can we check it out?"

"No touching."

Leo saluted and followed David around both machines. "Awesome. We'll be back later. Thanks."

Jim was just getting comfy on his cot when he heard the machine sputter. He threw his blanket off and ran to the main room with Dwight behind him. "What in the heck is going on?" The cave had filled with smoke.

"It's the generator. It's about to explode!"

"No, it isn't." But Jim wasn't sure of himself. He discovered the switch and powered down the machine. The smoke stopped. They walked out to get some fresh air. "So much for a new generator. We'll have to finish it up with the old one. Sad, it takes longer." He messed with the wire connecting to the machines. "Bring me the old one."

Dwight did as he was told.

"And call David. Tell him to meet us in the cornfield later.

"Okay."

Chapter 31

Missy felt nervous to see her old teammates at the harvest dance and hoped they weren't mad because she'd left without saying goodbye. She looked in her mirror, tucked and untucked her flannel shirt, and had difficulty deciding. The doorbell rang. She left the shirt untucked and went to answer it. "I'll get it."

She opened the front door and stared at the guy she loved. He loved her for who she was: crazy, spontaneous, and a believer in ghosts.

Brandon's eyes gleamed. "You're going for the cowgirl look, eh? I like you in your so-called tennis-shoe boots and hat. Come here." He flicked the edge of her hat and drew her to his lips.

She turned back and yelled, "I'm out of here, Mom! See you before midnight!"

"Bye and have fun. Drive carefully, Brandon. Those roads have no streetlights."

"Will do." He chuckled. "My mom said the same thing."

"A bunch of worrywarts, if you ask me."

"Why leave two hours early?"

Brandon headed to Missy's car, but she pulled him to his truck. "I'm driving but want your truck. It's safer for where we're going."

He gave her a questioning look.

"I don't want to be a backseat driver telling you where to turn. Plus, I know where the spot is. Please?" She expressed a pleading look. He passed over his keys.

"My gut's telling me I will not like this. What are you getting us into now?" He sat on the passenger side.

"A lot went on when I lived in Murphy. I hiked with Reed and by myself. He's looking for Starr, too. He supposedly has a box buried by his grave full of information and jewelry. Reed's mom is a descendant of Starr. The rest we know from reading about it at the library last year."

"I remember, along with the chilly breeze in the library's basement," Brandon said.

"Well, I want to explore a cave, check the box's presence, and find Starr's burial spot. She continued to tell Brandon more of what she and Reed had seen, her dreams, visions, the visits from Chief Tso'ape-ha, and the messages on the mirror and river.

"How do you stay calm?"

Missy exhaled. "I have no idea but want to show you the cave. I'm taking a chance of finding a closer place to park, so we aren't hiking on the train track."

Brandon raised his hands. "Always an exciting outing with my girlfriend."

She smiled and loved the sound of his statement. "To cure stress, I need a sugar rush."

"Sugar rush?"

Missy pulled into the gravel parking lot at Simply Made. She hoped Tricia didn't think she was a two-timer because she and Reed weren't an official boyfriend/girlfriend. "Homemade ice cream to die for."

"As you wish." Brandon followed her into the store. "Smells like a candy shop."

The bell rang, signaling customers, and Tricia walked around the divider. "Missy. How are you? It looks like you brought a guest. How's practice going?" She wiped her hands on her apron.

"I'm good, thank you. This is my boyfriend, Brandon, and I resigned from the team."

Tricia raised her eyebrows as if wanting more information. Missy gave none. "Well, nice to meet you, Brandon, and I wish you well on your new adventure, Missy. What can I get you?"

She and Brandon gave their orders and paid.

Leo and David entered, got their cones, and prepared to leave. "Hi." David offered his hand for a shake.

Missy recognized a faint smell of Twist, a scent she wished never existed.

Brandon accepted handshakes from both. "Nice to see you two."

"You guys heading for the party tonight?" Leo asked.

"Yes. You going?" Missy rubbed her thigh with her free hand and got the hint Brandon wanted to leave.

"We'll be there for part of it. Have other obligations to take care of." Leo winked at David.

"Great. It was nice seeing you. Bye." Missy moved around the guys so she and Brandon could get outside. After the door shut, she leaned over. "Those two are on Twist. I smelled it on their clothes."

"I knew the smell was off. You okay?"

"I have a sensitive nose, and it affects me quickly. I'm lightheaded, but it will leave soon. Hope the ice-cream helps." She straightened her back and licked the cone a few times. "Another reason my dreams of Jim are true. He's back making his drugs."

"I haven't heard my dad say a word, but as you know, he can't. He's only warned me not to go places he's worried about."

"He might not know this place. Reed, too, was in search of a drug hangout. I never smelled Twist when I was by him. I could be wrong, but maybe he's helping the local sheriff."

"Who knows." Brandon opened the driver's side door for Missy.

Driving past the entrance where she and Reed had walked, she silently prayed for guidance to make the right turn. She continued to tell Brandon all she'd gone through living at the Derringers', about Maura, Echo, where Reed hiked, and her map.

"I forgot the map at home. I don't know how, but I need to find out why I'm involved." They passed sporadic dirt roads until Missy had the sense to turn left on a narrow dirt road. "Hold on. The road looks bumpy."

"I better not get a flat tire." Brandon put his hands on the roof to hold himself steady.

A minute later, they pulled into a flat area to park by another car. "This is it." She got out of the truck along with Brandon.

"Where to now?" He walked to the edge of the hill.

"We go on the trail and search." She put the keys in her pocket.

"It doesn't look too steep." He took the first step.

Nope. "Been down it before without falling."

Missy and Brandon arrived at the spot she and Reed had discovered. Brandon scanned the hillside for an entrance. "Is this the place?"

She pointed more to the left. "There it is."

He looked around the desert hills surrounded by the Snake River. "Pretty."

"I can sit and listen to the river for hours. Ready?" She stepped up the small incline toward the cave.

"You think the box is still there?"

"The way to know is to look and hope for no visitors."

They entered the entrance and walked a few feet until the sunshine disappeared. They saw a slight glow at the corner of a turn in the cave's tunnel.

"A powerful flashlight or a battery-operated spotlight," Brandon said.

"I can smell Twist."

"You still want to check it out?"

"Maybe it's a group of school kids having a party," Missy offered.

"Only one way to find out."

In the first part of the cave, one machine was operating slowly sending plants through a heater. "This is how they make Twist." Missy nibbled on her free hand. She glanced sideways and saw the treasure box in its original state. "Should we grab it and leave?"

"You said it wasn't your problem."

"Maybe Reed forgot to tell his dad. I'm sure they'd love to have it." She headed to the box, touched the top, and yanked her hand off fast. "It's hot like on fire!" She blew on the tips of her fingers.

"How? There's no smoke or fire."

"I'm not sure, but water is what I urgently need." She turned and half-jogged to the river to soak her hand. Brandon followed.

"I'd still like to look around. There could be more caves up farther." She shook her hand to dry it off.

"Your hand cooled enough?"

"Yes." She explained how Reed wanted to follow Starr's ghost and find out where his grave was. No luck yet. "I need to come back. There's no time for hunting around." They walked back to the parking lot.

"Do you believe you saw the real Starr ghost?" They arrived at Brandon's truck.

She scrunched her face. "Don't you recall seeing the Native American chief in the tunnel? Are you saying you never believed in my nightmares and seeing Jim painted as a ghost driving the tractor in the field? You forgot?"

"I remember," Brandon assured her. "I don't want to get back into the ghost part or Jim and Dwight. It was an unpleasant situation for me and times one hundred for you. I'll ask my dad if he's heard of a rise in drugs. He arrested a few drug gangs, but there's still more to go."

"Let's join the party, be happy, and come back when we have more time." Brandon returned to the main road, and Missy directed him to the party. "We can explore farther and hike around on our next visit."

"Dang!" Brandon exclaimed. "We needed to get the license plate number from that other car. I have a feeling it will leave soon."

"I hope not. Someone's in there. Reed and I didn't get ten feet in before rocks were tossed at us."

Brandon moved his hands to a different spot on the steering wheel. She sensed he hesitated to ask or make a comment.

"What's wrong? Is your gut telling you that you have a crazy girlfriend? Or do you believe how I feel?" Missy didn't know if she should touch his arm while he drove.

"How serious were you with Reed?"

She scrunched her forehead. "What do you mean? You saw the quick kiss in the gym, and I can hold up one hand for the times we kissed. I know I'm not the first girl for you either."

He popped his lips. "Ally was spreading untrue rummers."

"Gosh darn her." She hit the seat hard. "Maura hardly said a peep about Ally. I told you about how she treated me. I hate her. What did she say? Or do I want to know?"

"I doubted what Ally said, but Kaleb loves to build a mountain of rumors about why you quit the team."

She was silent. No, she wouldn't let it get to her. She was past being a loser.

They drove back to the park where they saw several cars and people eating. Brandon turned and placed his hand on Missy's.

"I tried not to believe a word Kaleb told me about you two. But when you hear it every single day, it gets embedded in your mind. When you kept talking about your hikes with Reed," he moved his hand to her face, "it hurt because I was the stupid one to ignore you and break up."

"I get it, and I understand. It's always been you." She placed her hand on Brandon's. "Let's go have fun."

Echo saw Missy as she and Brandon got out of his truck and jogged to meet her. "I'm glad you came. I saved a spot by us at the picnic table." She hugged her and pointed behind her. "Come on. The chickens are ready to eat." She stopped for a second and smiled. "Oops, not the best way to introduce myself." She looked at the cute guy who stood by Missy. "This must be Brandon. I'm Echo." They reached the picnic table. "And this is Rich."

"Hi." Brandon offered a handshake to Rich.

"Nice to meet you again and, of course, we know Missy." Rich nodded.

"I'm starving, and the food smells delicious." Missy guided everyone to the barbecue, waving at her teammates as they called out to her. She was proud to have the best-looking guy by her side.

She glanced around while choosing her food at the table, hoping to spot Reed who was in the picnic's corner area talking to an unfamiliar girl. He noticed the stare, winked and continued his conversation with the girl and Bryce.

The two couples sat at the table and ate. Maura and Brett joined them. "Hi, people. Enjoying yourselves? What brings you back?" She sat across from Missy and acted like they were best buds.

"They invited me."

Maura looked back at Reed as if insinuating he had done it.

"I did because I missed Missy. She made me laugh all the time." Echo smiled.

"Run to the bathroom with me." Missy tabbed Echo's arm and looked at Brandon. "I'll be back." He nodded.

Echo stood and followed Missy. "What's wrong? I can tell you're flustered."

To avoid detection, Missy moved to the rear of the outhouse. "Do you think Sky's dead?"

"Whoa. Where did that question come from?"

"I'm going to summarize it, but think he moved me when I passed out by his cross. I smelled a fragrance coming from the holes in a closed cave in the mountains and woke up back down at the bottom. I also saw a homemade cave by the river close to the Bells' house. It could be his spirit or him in real life. Plus, I think I found the hidden box or one of them. It burned my hand when I touched it." She lifted her hand to see if any burned marks were present. None.

Echo nodded. "He's come back. I knew he wasn't dead. According to a friend, he was camping in the Washington Cascades. My beliefs remain uncertain. I mentioned before that Sky and I weren't on good terms."

"I remember and sorry." She hugged Echo, who returned the squeeze. "I have mixed feelings. Despite Reed's knowledge and his promise to inform his dad, the box remains. It puts more of a doubt on Reed telling me the truth about anything. Maybe he's one of the druggies for real and not pretending to help the police. Heck, even both coaches might be part of the drug dealing. I've seen Reed do a sale." Missy scratched the side of her head. "I hate asking, but do you think Sky is into drugs and helping the Bells?"

"I wouldn't be surprised if he was, though I hate to admit it," Echo said as she ended the conversation as the D.J. got on the microphone. "We can talk later on our own time."

"Get in a group of eight and form squares." The D.J. gave instructions as Missy and Echo returned to the table.

The program was a repeat of what they'd done for Halloween. In order were the square dance, line dance, and traditional dancing. Missy wasn't up to it.

Chapter 32

Jim stomped his foot after Missy and Brandon left the river. "That girl always sticks her nose where it doesn't belong. Perhaps we need to warn her about all the trouble she's causing." He stomped his other foot.

"How?" Dwight asked. "I'm woozy."

"Past normal?" Jim was on an anger roll. "I bet they'll be at the harvest dance. I'll hide out in the corn and grab her when she passes. Heck, we're meeting clients in the maze, so I'll be there ready for an attack."

He joined Dwight and watched the fresh herbs move into the baker on a belt. At the end of the heater was a bucket full of dried plants. With the bucket in hand, he moved it to a table alongside a box of small bags and a scale.

Dwight put more herbs on the belt. "David and Leo. Good bunch of kids."

Jim sniffed as the residue floated in the air. "Thanks to Reed. He's our best contractor. It makes him handle all his jobs better."

"It's possible he got Missy hooked on Twist to benefit the team."

Hands squeezed into fists, Jim raised his voice, "I hope she is, too, so it messes up her life like mine."

His mind splashed back to high school when their family's funeral home expanded underground to make their own drugs. He wished he'd had the right amount when he started going out with Violet. She was enjoyable company, but adding a hint of Twist would amplify the adventures. Unfortunately, Ray moved to town and disrupted everything. Jim wished he had stayed in Arizona, so he would have never met Violet, and his life might have been better.

He felt like running into the rock-caved wall but instead sniffed some Twist for stress relief.

Chapter 33

Missy pulled Brandon away. "Corn maze?"

"Sure." They walked a short distance to the main entrance.

"Should we divide and determine who reaches the exit first?" Brandon asked.

"No way, dude. What if I get lost, and a dragon breathing out fire wants to eat me? Perhaps a wicked witch will fly over the field and curse me with her wand."

"If a witch was flying around, I might want to see if she'd give free rides on her broomstick," Brandon teased.

Based on the same suggestions she had with Reed, she assumed all guys shared the same mindset. "If the seats are padded."

Brandon laughed. "Ready?"

"Lead the way, Sir Lancelot."

"Onward we go. Will any different paths in this maze lead you to the center or out?" Brandon took the lead.

"I'm told each year it's different. I've been here, but only know two exits. There are several more."

"Want to try a different trail you don't know?"

"If you'll be the compass, I'm game."

Brandon turned right, maneuvered through corn rows, and discovered an alternate route. They went around a corner and ran into Leo and David.

"Fancy bumping into you here." Leo's body swayed.

Missy knew he was high on Twist. "Sure is. I need to keep walking in order to get out. Bye." She snagged Brandon's hand and pulled him away. "They give me the creeps."

"I get ya." Brandon stepped in front of her. "I hear people talking, so I bet the center is close."

She stopped to listen, but Brandon disappeared around the corner. Missy went to catch up but stopped again when she heard the cornstalks move.

She turned, hoping it was Brandon, but saw Jim's face.

He yanked Missy behind the row of stalks. Still holding her arm, he put his free hand on her mouth and whispered, "You scream, and you're gone. Stop following me around. Stay away from me. If you don't, I'll give you nightmares that will make you wish you never went to sleep. Get my drift?" he threatened. "Why do you look like the lady I love?"

Missy tried to break free, and Jim pushed her back on the trail, where she landed on her side along with broken husks, dirt, and rocks. She knew he was under the influence of Twist but wasn't sure about the severity of his threat or the potential for violence. If she yelled, Jim might pull her back into the thickness of the cornhusks and strangle her. Her body shook, and she had a difficult time holding back the tears.

"Missy? Where are you? You lost?" Brandon walked back around the corner. He stopped when he saw her shivering and hugging her legs. He hurried to her side and squatted. "You fall?" He helped her stand.

"Get me out of here," she mumbled, unsure if she should speak to Brandon there. If she did, Jim could attack them both. It wouldn't be good if Jim had his drug buyers in the field with him- Leo and David. *I get why they're always happy.*

"You're shaking. Don't tell me you saw a dragon." He faked a laugh and tried to break the tension.

Missy rubbed the dirt off her left side as tears poured down her face. "He's here. He grabbed me and threatened I'd get hurt if I didn't leave him alone."

"Who's here?"

"Jim. He's hurt me for the last time." Brandon's arm muscles tensed against her body as he helped her walk.

Brandon stopped by the maze exit. "We have to tell my dad. Come on." He didn't question Missy on the ride back, and fortunately, none of their friends had seen them leave.

Halfway home, Missy wiped off her tears. "I feel like a crybaby."

"You're hardly that, Missy. I'm surprised the stupid guy is back."

"Why me? Why do we keep crossing paths? It's not like I'm stalking Jim. There's no connection."

Brandon drove as fast as possible without going over the speed limit. When he got enough bars on his cell, he called home. "Mom. Can you please call Missy's parents and have them over in fifteen minutes?"

"You bringing home extra dessert?"

"It's more like sour kraut," Brandon stated.

"You okay?"

"I'm fine, but Missy's not." The call ended.

"I hope after tonight, my visit to your home will be enjoyable." Missy leaned back against the headrest.

"It will happen."

"Why don't we call the sheriff in Murphy? Would it mess with your dad's job?"

"I'm not sure. Heck, the sheriff, or his employees, could also be dealers and covering the cave or other places nearby. Twist and other drugs have become popular in the last year. Some cops might be involved and helping the dealers."

Brandon pulled into his driveway and turned off the truck.

"Are you sure you're okay?" They could see Missy's parents through the window at his house. "I know my dad can't give us much information on this case, but we keep getting involved without trying to."

Missy let herself out of his truck and walked to the Millers' front door, hugging herself. She was quite aware of the state in which she must look. Her new hairstyle looked disheveled, as if she had crawled through dirt. Brandon ran ahead of her, opened the door, and called out to his parents. "Mom, Dad, bad news."

Missy's mother gasped in shock, composed herself, and hugged her daughter. She walked with her to the couch. "What happened? You fall off the hayride?"

"I got pushed." She leaned on her mom's shoulder. Her dad's face hardened.

"Trouble follows her like a magnet when it's least expected." Brandon shrugged.

Brandon's mom went to the kitchen, got a clean dishcloth, wrung out the water, and placed it on Missy's forehead.

Missy's father's comment sounded forced. "This reminds me of last year. You danced too much and got lightheaded. Or you got accidentally pushed on the ground on a square-dancing move." He stood by her and his wife.

"Jim. Jim pushed me." Missy wiped her face.

Her mom placed the back of her hand on Missy's cheek with a blank stare.

"Mom. I saw his face. He is my curse." She got up, headed to the bathroom, splashed water on her face and returned to the couch.

"Brandon and I know where they're hiding because I snooped around. At the party, we ventured through the corn maze, and Jim expected my presence. He pulled me off the trail when Brandon was ahead of me. He put his hand over my face and squeezed me hard." She rubbed the arm Jim had hurt and she had fallen on.

"Jim said to mind my own business and leave him alone, or I'd be gone. He'd take care of me. He told me not to scream. I always freeze when surprised or scared, but I tried to get out of his grip. Jim noticed I was defending myself, pushed me back through the cornstalks onto the path, and I landed on my side. I didn't scream because he could have dragged me back into the field and hurt me worse."

Missy's dad paced back and forth in the front room and, to Missy, it looked like smoke was steaming out of his ears. "Jim needs to burn."

"Jim? He died last year." Mrs. Mack hugged Missy and caressed her hair.

"No, Mom. He got away."

Brandon and his mom stood, not knowing what to do. Mr. Miller stepped into the kitchen and called headquarters. He briefly described what Missy had told them and where Jim was last seen. Mr. Miller confirmed he'd have Missy look at a map and point out where the cave was. Returning to the family room, he directed his attention toward Missy. "It's always hard reliving what you've gone through, but since it's fresh in your mind, I need every confrontation you had with Jim."

She nodded and pulled herself from her mom's arms.

"Currently, the Owyhee Gymnastic Team has two users," she mentioned, "and there might be more."

"What are their names?"

"Leo and David."

After an hour of discussing Brandon's side of the cave story and what they witnessed, Missy pinpointed the area on a map between Murphy and Silver City.

The next day, in the early evening, Mr. Miller gave the news to the Macks. The cave was found, and part of The Rock's Edge gang was present. A fight ensued, not unlike many that Mr. Miller had experienced before. In the end, they'd arrested all except for Jim and Dwight, who were, unfortunately, not in the cave along with a half-buried treasure chest.

Chapter 34

"I told myself no more procrastination buying Christmas gifts." Missy stood by Julie in line at Ice Scream You Scream.

"We have a couple of weeks until Christmas Day."

"Last year I bought my gifts on the twenty-third. Not much to choose from."

"I remember."

Missy squinted her eyes. "I feel a little funny."

"Ears ringing?"

"No, different. Like someone's watching me."

"Not this again. Is Starr riding his horse in the mall's walkway?" Julie asked.

After they ordered their ice cream, the girls sat in a booth. Reed, Brett, and a person Missy didn't know arrived. She looked at Julie. "I figured out why I had butterflies in my stomach."

Julie glanced and licked the side of her cone covered with melting ice cream. "Why?"

"He can't see me."

"Who can't see you?"

"Reed."

"*Achoo*." Julie didn't help by sneezing. "Excuse me."

"You did that on purpose." Missy gave Julie the eye.

"Nuh-uh."

It caught Reed's attention. His face brightened, and he whispered to his friends and came over to their table. "Missy. How are you?"

She wasn't sure what to do—stand or stay seated. Missy held out her hand. "Hi."

He pulled her up for a bear hug. Last thing she wanted was Brandon to walk in during their hug not knowing his reaction. *Would a fight start?*

Reed loosened his hold and stepped back. "You look great."

"Thank you. How are you, Brett?" She looked at the unknown visitor.

He patted the guy's back. "This is my brother, Bryan. And before you ask, Maura is Maura. I knew the question was bouncing around in your brain."

"Whatever." She laughed. "What brings you to the mall in Nampa?"

"Meeting with a leasing agent, and this is the center point." Reed glanced at his friends. "We're planning on opening a gymnastics team here—the Treasure Valley Gymnastics Team." Reed looked at his cell. "We can't be late." The guys stood. "Nice seeing you, Missy. Bye, Julie."

"Fun. I hope it works out." Missy side-eyed Julie as they left.

"I can't believe I ran into Reed, and I didn't believe a word he said."

"I thought you didn't like him."

"Not for sure now. He triggers an uneasy feeling."

"Are you going on your rampages again about new ghosts or premonition stuff?"

Missy ignored Julie's stab and stood. "I'm going to follow. You are more than welcome to come." She licked her cone, faced the shop entrance, and waited for Julie. "Hurry. I have to know their destination." She stepped forward and gasped.

"Missy, you look like you're going to faint." Julie leaned over to observe people walking by on the main walkway.

"He's here." Missy pointed out of the store. "Come on."

"What? Who's here?" Julie shook her arm out of Missy's hand.

"My nightmare." They watched Jim go past the restrooms and exit the parking lot. She noticed Reed and his followers heading in the same direction right after he turned. "They're meeting."

"It could be a coincidence. Jim wouldn't know Reed."

It's no coincidence that two guys on the team purchased from Jim. Now it looks like the entire team's on drugs." They followed Jim's invisible footprints and watched them all go out into the parking lot. Missy opened the exit door a crack. Reed, Brett, Bryan, and Jim stood in a circle. Dwight got out of a parked car and joined them. The conversation seemed calm.

"What if they fight? I'd like to see Reed punch the living heck out of Jim."

"You seem obsessed with him; all he gives you is problems."

"Not. I want to know what they're talking about. Reed took me on all the hikes to find unknown places to hide drugs, and I'm not surprised he's a dealer or a maker." Missy shrugged.

"I don't believe it. Your life seemed chaotic, but this tops it all, and I don't know what to say." Julie closed the door in silence. "It's time to go."

"I agree one hundred percent. Please drop me off at Brandon's."

Julie drove Missy to her destination, but she couldn't get the feeling she'd had in the parking lot out of her mind. Something bad was happening, and she knew Brandon would help. "Hugs, dear friend, and I hope all is figured out soon."

Missy returned the hug. "Thanks, me too," she said and waved as she got out.

Brandon opened the front door as she approached. "Come on in. I'm helping Mom pull the baseboards off in the family room."

"Sounds fun." She attempted to appear cheerful.

"Hi, Missy. Hope all's going well." Brandon's mom greeted her and went to the garage to get more paste.

"I've seen that look before. Now what?" Brandon asked.

Missy didn't get a chance, as Brandon's dad, on his cell, walked into the kitchen. "Twist is making a comeback in Kuna, Melba, and the surrounding area. Our men should be positioned in the marked areas." He walked into the living room to see the progress as Brandon and Missy stared back. "Thank you for the information, and I'll get back to you." He clicked the off button. "You didn't hear my conversation."

Missy went stone-faced.

"I see you did."

Missy looked at Brandon as his mom came back. "Trouble?" She put the bucket on the tarp.

"Looks like Missy has some information to share," Mr. Miller said.

"I saw Jim again at the mall a half hour ago. He was in the parking lot with a few of the Owyhee gymnastics team."

"He's still here. Do you have more?" Mr. Miller asked.

"I came here to tell Brandon, but I had to inform you," she replied. "I know who works with him. There's a hiding place he uses in or near Nampa. I can feel it."

Missy sat on the couch. "Want me to call my parents this time?"

"I called them in the garage. They're walking up the driveway now." Mrs. Miller opened the front door.

"Hello." Missy's dad shook Mr. and Mrs. Miller's hands. "It seems like this warrants a gathering."

Mr. Miller told everyone to sit in the family room. "I need to record our conversation if that's okay. It's part of the procedure. This is confidential information."

"You're telling us our kids were at the wrong place at the wrong time again?" Missy's dad's expression was confused.

"It's about drugs, but only the connections. Our kids are fine, but like magnets, drawing in trouble." He pointed at Missy. "Go ahead."

"I went with Julie to the mall and met Reed, Brett, and his brother Bryan, who isn't on the team. They saw us in the ice cream store and sat. Reed mentioned meeting a property manager to explore a site for a new gymnastics facility. I saw right through it. A few minutes later, Jim walked by. I followed and saw them talking in the parking lot, and Dwight arrived in a car. He's stupid for not leaving after his Murphy cave was discovered. His brain is dead." Missy grinded her teeth. "He has greatly affected both my mind and life." She leaned on her mom's shoulder.

"Any more information?"

"No." Missy sniffed.

The Macks looked at each other.

Brandon's dad put his notebook on an end table and turned off the recorder. "I previously told you both to stay away from certain areas, but now it's irrelevant because you're not going to forbidden places. Please be careful and don't follow." He looked at Missy and tapped his fingers on the notebook. "If you see Jim, find a secluded place and let us where you are. Call me."

He waved his cell to Missy. "I have more work to do." He turned to the Macks. "Thank you for coming over. I don't like it, but we are all involved."

Missy's parents got ready to leave and gestured for her to follow. She stood with the glass in her hand. "Can I talk to Brandon for a minute?" Brandon glanced for a second before he looked elsewhere.

They nodded and Mrs. Miller took the glass from Missy and placed it in the sink. With the two alone, Missy touched Brandon's arm. "I need to talk to you, but let's go somewhere else."

"Don't be long." Brandon's mom said.

"We won't." Missy followed her parents as they walked out the front door. "I'm not trying to cause trouble. I promise."

"We know, but roaming around needs to be slim until the case ends."

Missy waved as her parents left.

"Around the block?" Brandon asked as they reached the end of the driveway.

"I want to go to the shack."

"You hate the shack. And it's going where we shouldn't."

"It's been close to a year, and there's no yellow tape wrapped around it." Missy tried to justify her request.

"Whatever." Brandon's expression was natural, but Missy knew he was edgy as they headed to where Jim once slept between diggings in the field during the night. After they arrived at the shack, they noticed the old cot, the small desk, and chair were still there. The police covered and blocked the hole in the underground tunnel. The framed newspaper article about Jim's accident lay crumbled on the floor.

Brandon looked confused. "A lot happened when I lived in Murphy," Missy paced back and forth. "You mentioned having a girlfriend prior to moving here but didn't elaborate on the seriousness of the relationship. I could tell you still cared about her. You still could, for all I know. At the first of this last school year, you avoided me. I felt betrayed and didn't understand why until recently." She glanced at Brandon before resuming her pacing. "I heard later that Sarah sat by you as a tag-along. Funny, I was jealous even after we got back together." She sat on the cot. "As I told you, I liked Reed because I knew you and I were done. You were tired of me."

"Tired of you? I couldn't get enough of you, and it scared me to picture you and Reed walking in the dark. It's not my business to know your personal life. We weren't together."

"I can tell you're hurt."

"And when Reed kissed you?" He shook his head.

"It hurt me, too, when I saw you." Missy wiped away another tear. "Brandon, nothing happened between Reed and me. I told you before, but I still know you doubt what Maura told Ally. Please believe me. Four or five kisses. He hardly held my hand. I don't know, but I want to erase it from my mind. Running into Reed twice and seeing Jim causes me to think I helped Reed find places to hide drugs, including Twist, and a new area to make it." Missy turned to face her boyfriend. "I love you, Brandon Miller."

He took a few seconds to reply. "I wasn't nice because I feared unfamiliar feelings. I got you in trouble in the tunnel, and you ran into Jim. If he sees you again, who knows what he'll do? We can't even be free in Nampa without looking behind us to ensure he isn't following. And yes, when you talked more about living in Murphy, I wondered how serious you'd gotten with Reed. I also felt hurt and jealous."

"You, jealous? You could get any girl you wanted."

He hugged Missy for reassurance. "Nobody is close to you, and I hope Reed and Jim won't cause problems."

"I'll make sure of it."

Chapter 35

"Missy still on your mind?" Brett inquired Reed while they strolled to the mall's other side.

"How can you tell?" Reed leaned against the building's wall.

Jim approached a parked car Dwight got out of. They headed back to where Reed and his friends gathered.

"It's all over your face."

"History. All games now," He assured Brett.

"Bull crap. You always talked about Missy when she lived at Maura's house."

Reed shrugged. "I'm sure it would be different if she'd stayed in Murphy. However, Missy didn't, and life moves forward. I'm surprised you're still with Maura."

"Me too."

"Me three," Bryan said. "All you do is complain about her manipulation and cold-heartedness. What made you interested in Missy? To me, she's okay looking. She doesn't stand out like Maura."

"It was the look of trouble. I felt a powerful urge to assist her. We have a few subjects of mutual interest."

"Like school classes?"

Reed didn't want to explain the whys to his friend. He wasn't in the mood to explain his decisions to anyone.

Fortunately, Jim and Dwight showed up and he didn't have to.

Chapter 36

Mixed emotions had troubled Missy nonstop since last Saturday. She didn't have nightmares, but a nagging feeling she needed to go somewhere. The problem was, she couldn't point out where until Tommy watched *Indiana Jones and the Raiders of the Lost Ark* on Saturday morning instead of cartoons.

Missy left without her mom's approval, mentioning she was going to Brandon's house. On her way, she dreamed.

She'd gone for a joy ride back to Murphy to another barbecue and dance party in full swing. The scenery transformed as she stepped out of the car, returning to the closed cave in the mountains. Finding an opening, Missy ventured into the cave to find a table among her friends.

"How strange to have a party in the cave." Missy scratched her head. It was dark and hard to see. Lights turned on in front of her, and she saw the table. She took a step closer, but a familiar noise halted her.

A tractor revved its engine. She turned and ran with the tractor on her tail. The ghost, Jim, who was driving, laughed. "Oh, boy, this is fun. Doesn't it bring back memories, Missy?" The tractor's front bumped the backs of Missy's feet. "I'm back!"

"Earth to Missy. You sleepwalking?" Still in dreamland, she stood at the front door of Brandon's before realizing he stared back.

She looked at her boyfriend as if she'd never seen him before, then shook her head. "I got it. I know what we need to do." She touched his chest and pushed him back into his house. "Get your keys. We're going for a drive."

Brandon's mom sipped her hot tea. "You're up bright and early. Going out for breakfast?"

"Yes. Yes, we are," Missy said.

Brandon shrugged. "Surprise plan for me. I'm game." They left and got in his truck. "Where to?"

"I guess eating first is good. I am getting hungry; go to BF."

"Murphy? You going to tell me why?" He backed out of the driveway.

"I want to return to the cave I mentioned with that distinct smell."

"Why?"

"Tommy was watching *Indiana Jones and the Raiders of the Lost Ark*. It fits my life. The story does. To safeguard buried secrets or treasures from the bad guys, someone responsible should either leave them alone or hand them over." She told Brandon about her vision on the walk to his house, and how the dreams from the last couple of weeks differed from her nightmares.

Brandon pulled into the dirt parking lot at BF. In the back, they saw Reed sitting on the hood of his car. "I don't want to disturb a show."

"This will prove he's selling drugs." Missy leaned forward for a closer look. Bad idea. Reed glanced at Brandon's truck. "I hope he can't see through the window. The sun is beaming on it."

"He isn't leaving. Should we go or not?" Brandon questioned uncertainly.

"No. Let's stay." She messed with Brandon's cell.

A few minutes later, a truck drove in and parked by Reed. "Time to record a trade. How do you work this recording?" Missy asked.

Brandon took his cell and recorded Leo and David standing by Reed, who handed them a small bag. In return, Leo gave Reed cash.

"They're busted. Can your dad use this information?"

"I don't know. Each case is different in how it's handled, and we are in Owyhee County. My dad is located in Canyon County."

Leo and David left, and Reed went into BF. "It will be a weird situation, but I'm hungry and need to act normal."

"Good luck. I'm scared as heck." Brandon locked his truck. "I'm going to call and ask. Go in and order. Get me whatever." Brandon turned and headed toward the back of his truck.

My stomach's sick. What do I say to Reed? He knows I saw him. Okay, here it goes. She saw Reed at the counter. Since it was a seat yourself café, she chose the booth by the door. If he looked, it wouldn't matter. The café's door had a bell.

Reed paid for his to-go order and acted like Missy wasn't there until he got by her booth. "Now it's your turn to see me in my town. Reason?" Reed asked.

"I was hungry."

He closed his eyes a couple of seconds longer than expected. "Do you miss me? Are you happy?"

"Your reason to go to the mall was to take a chance of running into me?" Missy kept her knowledge of his encounters with Jim and Dwight a secret, wondering if that explained his frequent visits to the mall.

Reed hadn't expected a comeback. He stared Missy in the face. "Look, I told you the partial truth when we went hiking and looking for Starr's burial place. There's more, and I can't say it." He moved his tongue around in his mouth with his lips closed. "I know I can trust you."

"I'm sure you can sense you're putting pressure on me to guess what you want to tell me."

"You've changed," Reed said.

Missy lifted her hands up in confusion.

"You've turned into a Maura."

"How? It's getting warm in here." Missy flapped her hand to fan her face. I've learned not to be taken advantage of. Second. I still have feelings for you, but not enough to end my current relationship. Third." *Crap.* Missy clenched her fists. "I know what you're doing and the person you met with at the mall." She ran her fingers through her hair. "The question is to you. Are you now a drug dealer and helping Jim do his work?"

Reed ignored the question. "I like you more than casually." He looked toward the waitress, hesitating by the cash register to give the glass of water to Missy. Reed nodded.

The waitress placed the glass on the table and asked if she was ready to order.

"I'll take two of the specials." Missy didn't know or care what it was.

"Good choice." She returned with a pitcher of water and an extra cup. "Shout if you need anything else."

"Thanks, I will." Missy glared back at Reed. "You're avoiding my question."

"I'll answer your questions after I ask you one. How do you know Jim?"

She bit her upper lip and hoped Brandon would enter soon. "How could you? I never thought you'd lower yourself to using drugs."

A look of fear covered Reed's face as if he knew he and his family were in deep trouble. "I'm clean. Promise." His voice raised a notch.

"It doesn't look like it. You can't tell me anything else?"

He cocked his head. "Look. I took you on possible unsafe trails." He paused.

"I for one, don't want to get involved with anyone drug-wise," Missy finished. "You used me to search with you for Starr's hidden box. It was all a hoax, then? The buried box wasn't full of drugs or Starr's treasures your mom wants. It was an excuse to have me there."

"No. It's true. You saw the box."

She shook her hand. "Fake. I bet like a play. Stage prop." Missy knew the truth, but concealed her knowledge from Reed.

He glanced at Brandon as he opened the door.

"Nice running into you," Reed said. "You know, the team misses you." He nodded to Brandon as he left.

Missy glanced at him briefly before her attention shifted to Brandon.

Brandon sat. "I felt the heat."

"Reed was very uncomfortable. He or his dad might be the bad boys."

"Nothing makes sense," Brandon shook his head.

"No kidding."

"Have you had time to order?"

"Yes. What did your dad say?" Missy asked.

The waitress returned with their food. "Ketchup, Tabasco sauce?"

Missy nodded.

Brandon added salt and pepper to his eggs. "He thanked me for the information, but that's all for us. He'll inform the local sheriff's office and take it from there. If trouble gets out of hand, Dad will do his stuff."

He spread jam on his toast. "What did Reed say?"

"He was just adding more unmatching pieces to the puzzle. He knows something but can't tell me though he said he was clean."

"I'm starting to mistrust anything Reed says," Brandon admitted.

She told him the rest as they finished their breakfast. "A connection to the cave must exist."

"True, and he could've led you into a dangerous situation out in the woods. If I run into Reed again, I'll punch him in the face."

Missy ignored his comment knowing it was his way to protect her. "Can I borrow your cell, please?" She dug in her bag to look for a piece of paper with Echo's number. "Found it."

He handed her his cell. "Who are you calling?"

She held up her hand and punched the numbers.

"Echo? Hi, this is Missy. I know this is short notice, but can you meet me at the main bridge? Say thirty minutes?" Missy fiddled with her fork on the plate. "Please bring Vallie, too. I'll explain everything when we meet."

Chapter 37

Missy's heart raced as they approached the familiar bridge with the wooden planks. She rubbed her thighs as a stark reminder of her first visit and the mysterious message left on the river. "I so hope this aligns with my plans," she murmured, more to herself than to Brandon.

He parked his truck and cast a curious glance her way. "And what might those plans be?"

She flashed a wry smile, "The ones I'll figure out once we find an opening to the cave or create our own." Climbing out of the truck, she stretched her legs and felt the anticipation build. Echo and Vallie pulled in, their arrival punctuating the quiet of the forest. "Hey, thanks for indulging on one of my impromptu escapades," Missy greeted them, her voiced tinged with gratitude.

Leaning against their car, Echo raised an eyebrow. "Embarking on a new trail today?"

"I found a hidden trail that leads to Sky's cross"

"What? Sky has a cross?" Vallie put her hands on her chest. "Has he been here all this time?"

"I doubt it. I suspect he left it there as an escape plan, in case he's still alive." Echo made a face. "He's been gone for years."

Missy gave her friend a hug. "I believe this is the final piece of the puzzle. The one that will unravel the mysteries of Murphy's tangled web."

"Murphy is small with family links like a soap opera. Some people keep to themselves, while others dig deep for any answers." Echo's words hung in the air, a somber reflection on their small town's intricate connections. "I regret not forging a bond with Sky," she confessed, her gaze dropped to the ground.

Missy compared her statement to Reed. Was she talking about him? She paused and turned to face her friends. "I'm pretty sure this will help the whys. And I'm sad you didn't have a good relationship with Sky."

"Me, too. I'm sadder because I know it was my fault for not liking him and feel it was one reason he left." They reached the small boulder to climb up.

Brandon was quiet during the conversation and had stepped back to not interfere. He was like a ghost; nobody knew he was there until he spoke. "I'll stay behind to catch any slips on the climb up the boulder."

"I'm sorry for not saying hi." Echo touched his hand before she climbed.

He acknowledged and returned the hello to the sisters. "I'm here for support." Missy hugged him and put her feet in the boulder's holes.

Vallie looked around, "How did you find the covered path to the cross?"

Missy indicated the sturdy oak, her companion during the fateful event. "I sat and leaned against this tree. I dozed off and the squirrels playing around woke me. A wildcat ran in front of me, disappeared and triggered my imaginative brain."

Brandon's smile was a silent acknowledgment of Missy's whimsical thoughts.

"There's more to the story," she continued, her voice a blend of determination and wonder. "After discovering Sky's cross, I knew there was a deeper truth waiting to be unearthed."

As they trekked the forgotten path, the weight of their quest settled upon them. The cross loomed ahead, a sentinel amidst the rugged terrain, beckoning them closer with its silent call. Vallie jogged to the cross, squatted, and ran her fingers over his name. "I'm patiently waiting for Sky to whisk me away to a magical realm."

Echo joined her sister. "I hope his was a real trip, not a drug trip." She indicated the mountain's right side near the cross. It was a steep cliff. "Unless our cave dweller is adept at scaling sheer cliffs, I doubt we'll find an entrance."

Missy went behind the cross to the mountain's side. "Look. There has to be away. There are manmade air holes. I don't think nature caused it."

Brandon joined and peeked through one. "You're right. I see an open space." Each sister found and looked through an opening. "I don't see anything but smell a light fragrance."

"The two times I was here, I smelled an herbal fragrance. The sensation made me fall asleep initially, and upon waking, I was back down on the ground by the tree. Someone carried me away from here."

"Did you fall asleep on the second visit?" Brandon asked.

Echo interrupted. "Did you come back by yourself?"

"No. I was with Reed who was unaware of my visit. He looked into one hole and smelled the fragrance. I left feeling dizzy and didn't want to faint again." Missy didn't dare look at Brandon knowing his expression would be one of questioning.

Echo pressed her lips and Vallie looked clueless but put on a positive reply. "I have faith the other side will reveal its secrets."

"Let's see if there's an entrance to the left." Missy took the lead.

"I'm up for it. You?" Vallie pointed at Echo who looked hurt. Brandon still kept quiet but stayed close enough to Missy to provide any type of protection.

The trail led them away from the mountain, and Missy lost hope. "I'm pleading it goes toward the mountain and not the opposite direction. If this doesn't solve any problems, I will isolate myself for the rest of my life or finish making holes by the cross." Missy looked at Brandon, who shrugged. She didn't blame him one bit and crossed her fingers he wouldn't drop her for good after the wild goose chase, she'd put him through.

The path curved back to the mountain's side and there nestled in the stone, an opening beckoned. "I see an opening." She waited for the rest to catch up. Echo touched the edge and Missy saw a look of fear cross her face. "Are you scared of ghosts or the enclosed cave?"

Echo averted her stare, seemingly embarrassed by the attention. "I dread the thought of facing my presumed-dead brother. What if he resents me for my coldness?" Her voice trembled and revealed the guilt gnawing at her. She straightened up and glanced at Vallie. "Please forgive me."

Vallie reached out, her expression softening. "You can't blame yourself. It was his choices and his friends who drove him away, not you."

Echo shook her head in disbelief.

A heavy silence fell over the group, broken only but Missy's firm voice who held onto Brandon's hand for support. "Hold on, both of you. Let's pivot for a moment. I've been pondering something crucial. Are you linked to Starr, a distant relative?"

Echo's lips curled into a half-smile. "Not at all, though I understand the confusion with our nature-inspired names. Our father embraced the 'Nature-Loving Hippy' ethos of the '70s."

"Sorry for asking, but that takes weight off my back."

"No problem." She stared back at the entrance. "I always felt my brother wasn't dead, and it makes me sad he disowned himself from the family."

Vallie hugged her big sister. "Shall we venture inside?"

"You're the brave one, Missy." Echo gestured toward the dark entrance.

Brandon activated his cell's dim flashlight, and the two sisters followed suit. Missy took cautious steps, her eyes scanning the uneven ground. They rounded a corner into a small clearing where light filtered through the handmade holes, illuminating a semi-flat rock. Atop it sat a glass jar filled with dried herbs and three locked boxes side by side. Rusted locks held their grip tight so no one could open them without a struggle except for one, which looked familiar.

"That's the one we saw in the cave by the river. Did Reed bring it here?" Missy mused aloud.

"I'm in the Twilight Zone. Nothing makes sense," Echo frowned.

Her comment shocked Missy, but she didn't blame her. Trouble was her shadow. With no return reply, she asked an important question. "What are we supposed to do? Leave it be, call the cops, open the treasure chests? Search for more boxes? Forget none of this happened?" She desired the latter but understood it was impossible. "Tell your dad or the local authorities?" Missy squeezed Brandon's hand.

Their debate was interrupted by the sound of footsteps and a voice. "I've scoured the lands once roamed by Starr Wilkinson, the infamous outlaw."

Echo and Vallie spun around to face the newcomer. "Sky. Is it you?" Vallie sprung forward and threw herself into his arms for a hug. "You're alive. You're not dead." Her cries echoed inside the cave. "But why, why did you leave?" She tightened her hug.

Missy and Brandon were lost in their words. Echo stared at her brother who still embraced her sister and gave him a single nod. He set Vallie free and lovingly welcomed Echo for a hug. "Come here."

She hesitated for a second and rushed into his arms. "I'm so sorry I pushed you away. Please forgive me. Please." She released a suppressed cry, like a volcano erupting.

"It's fine. You did nothing wrong. I, with a stubborn mind, believed I could change the world. I made some poor decisions, but changed my ways and now am helping to save history." He pulled his sisters in closer forgetting there were two other people standing in the corner. "I know the connection between Starr W. and Mrs. Bell, plus the drug dealers."

Missy couldn't hold back. "So, you are doing the opposite of Reed? Chaundra wants any connection to Starr, and you don't think she can, have it? What gives you the authority to make the rules?"

Sky stepped away from his sisters and stood by the table rock. "I'm doing what needs to be done. History needs to stay buried."

"Chief Tso'ape-ha," Missy whispered as she remembered his visit to her on the bridge with the same warning.

He appeared confused, but Echo turned to her friends. "My goodness, how rude of me not to introduce you." Her voice sounded lost. "This is Missy, an exceptional gymnast, and her boyfriend, Brandon."

Brandon and Sky shook hands and did the general 'Nice to meet you.' Next, he shook Missy's hand and a sudden spark entered her palm; she felt a strange feeling like his spirit was talking to her spirit. It was a connection. Lost in the moment, she didn't hear another person join the group.

"Well, well, if it isn't the prodigal brother. I had a hunch you'd resurface." Reed's voice cut through the tension.

Sky met Reed's gaze, unflinching. "You've been scavenging for my remains?"

"Indeed. And I see you've been busy," Reed remarked, eyeing the treasure boxes with a mix of admiration. "Just one left to uncover."

"Your mom still wants to open and keep all the treasures?"

"Unfortunately, yes. But I'm with you. I play my part in their charade."

Missy watched the exchange like a verbal tennis match. Reed's revelation about his double life left her reeling. "Then, why are you dealing drugs?" She raised her arms. "I saw you more than once. You said you were clean and proved me wrong this morning. Was it you leaving arrowheads to mark places to meet with Twist buyers?"

Brandon moved behind Missy and put his hands on her shoulders. The feeling calmed her enough to not strike. "You used me to find hidden so-called treasure. Our secrets may be intertwined, but I'm done being a pawn in your game."

Reed and Sky exchanged glances as Echo and Vallie looked lost. "Let me explain," Reed started.

"No. How did you get the box here without your hands burning?" She felt her face getting hot in anger.

"I didn't move it and pretty sure it wasn't my dad. Don't think he knows about this cave."

Sky butted in. "I did, and it didn't burn my hands."

"Why? I can't comprehend the hidden secrets in the boxes, their mysterious senses, and their knowledge of who can touch them. But why not you?" Missy rubbed her hands together. "And why am I involved?"

"You got me there on your involvement but the point is, Starr W wants his boxes together and buried for good. Not sure he wants items removed."

"How do you know?"

"I'd rather not say."

Missy sensed Sky, too, had spiritual visits and nodded. "I have to find the answers on my own terms. How, where, and when? At this moment, we don't need each other's help," she shrugged. "I'm out of here." She grabbed Brandon's hand and pulled him out of the cave.

Outside, the snow began to fall, and Missy's tears mingled with the delicate flakes. She felt overwhelmed, buried under the weight of revelations and betrayals. A chilling scream echoed from the cave, halting their retreat. "Should we check on them?" Missy felt torn between concern and the desire to flee.

Brandon zipped up his jacket. "No. Whatever's happening in there is supernatural or just plain human folly; it's not your battle anymore."

They continued their escape, the cold biting at their skin. Missy sought reassurance from Brandon. "Do you still care for me; despite the chaos I've dragged you into?"

His embrace was her answer, warm and unwavering. "I'm as lost as you are in the crazy hidden secrets combining people from your past. Reed, Jim, Starr, and now Sky. Blows my mind, but it's their problem." They reached his truck, and he opened the door for Missy.

"I need to discover the reason for my connection." Missy crossed her fingers he wouldn't want to break up. He proved her wrong.

"Your life isn't a problem for me," he assured her. "Your mind isn't crazy and I still love you. I'm sure there's a link to connect the dots, and we'll unravel this mystery side by side."

"One more thought." She stopped him from closing the truck door. "What if Jim returns, haunting my life like a ghost?"

"We'll cross that bridge when we come to it, but if his brain is partially functional, he'll know to stay far far away," his tone was a blend of determination and hope. "For now, let's focus on the path ahead."

Missy's series continues with book three, Secrets Revealed, release date, in January 2025

J.S. Andersen other books:

Hidden Secrets:
https://www.goodreads.com/book/show/34677706-hidden-secrets

Buried Secrets:

My Poetic Soul:
https://www.amazon.com/MY-POETIC-SOUL-J-Andersen-ebook/dp/B07RVHJ8N9/

Facebook:
https://www.facebook.com/jsmithandersen/
https://www.facebook.com/melissamackadventure/

Blog:
http://jsandersen.allauthor.com/
https://jeanettesandersen.blogspot.com/

Twitter:
https://twitter.com/snapgrowl

LinkedIn:
https://www.linkedin.com/in/jsmithandersen/

Made in United States
Troutdale, OR
11/01/2025